Truth be Told

By

Justine Johnston Hemmestad

First Edition Published by Faith by Grace Publishing

First Faith by Grace Publishing Printing 2015.

The historical figures in this book are real but their stories are fictitious. All work is from the imagination of the author.

ISBN-13: 978-0692627686

ISBN-10: 069262785

A record of the Library of Congress serial number can be acquired from the publisher.

Manufactured in the United States of America

Cover done by Bradley Max Hemmestad

Edited by Paul Ewart

With Special Thanks To

My Grandfather Max and my Step-father Roger for supporting me in my writing and education.

Late 11th Century, England

My mind drifted to thoughts of my betrothed Arnulf, Earl of Pembroke, as I leaned out of a balcony window in the Norman castle built in the name of his father's commander and king, William. Though King William had conquered England many years ago, there were still strongholds among the Welsh. I awaited Arnulf's return from battle at one of those strongholds now. Though I was younger than him by almost fifteen years, my heart soared as I thought of the unity and order he brought to a region where once only chaos had abounded. His knights helped him fight for order throughout the land, in the name of God and country. I would soon be his wife, and I knew that my safety and future were things I would always embrace. Though I had heard the rumor of his, and his brother's, cruelty with their enemies, I did not believe it. Yet my betrothed was as obscure to me as on the day I was introduced to him, for his heart and his power often blinded me with wisdom.

I gazed upon the gardens below, their red and yellow flowers ever graceful in the bright sunlight that embellished what was already beautiful. A sudden and loud knock upon my bedroom door abruptly removed me from my peaceful thoughts. I bolted back from the window and turned toward the dark wooden door, dashing toward it and quickly opening it. A knight I knew called Sir Christoff stood on the other side, his hair gray beside his ears, his face aged by the sun, and his figure solid and armored in chainmail. "My Lady," he urgently began, "the Earl has been injured in battle."

I heard myself scream, but as though I were in a dream. I then found myself firmly cradled in the strong arms of the knight, though the room around me went black. Several moments had passed before I woke up inside a gently-driven carriage. Red velvet curtains with gold tasseled ties upon the window reminded me of my royal station in spite of my confusion. I struggled to sit up and peek outside to see the knight in whose arms I had fainted, fully armored in chainmail and riding his dark horse beside the carriage.

"Sir Christoff," I called to him, my voice revealing my lack of strength. He peered toward me, the chainmail armor shifting without unsettling the pace of his horse. "Where are you taking me?" I questioned as regally as I could manage. "Where is the Earl?"

He peered to me, his eyes hollow in what I interpreted as sadness. He answered, "We are going to Lord Arnulf now."

"Is he hurt terribly?" I questioned, my voice trembling with fear.

"The message I delivered is the message I was sent to deliver," he said. A second knight reined his horse up directly beside him. The rider peered through me, into my soul, so intrusively that I wondered if I had known him from somewhere before and I should have recognized him.

"Who are you?" I asked the newly-approached knight, whom was also armored in a suit of chainmail with a red, draping vest and royal crest upon his chest.

"I am Sir Lawrence," he answered with a sly grin, his dark eyes twinkling with an unspoken humor and his shoulders broad beneath his armor. "Lord Arnulf awaits in a village near Pembroke. We go to meet him now." My brow tensed with his words, but he added, "You will learn of the Earl's health once we arrive."

I turned to Sir Christoff again and he looked also to me. "Does the Earl not value truth above all else," I challenged.

"Quite so, my Lady," Sir Lawrence answered. But before I could say anything in return, something as powerful as a clap of thunder pierced the carriage. An arrow had embedded itself into the door beside my head. My mouth opened in horror. I could not breathe; nor could I move; nor could I scream.

"Stay inside!" Sir Christoff shouted. I dared not raise my head to see him. My eyes were closed so tightly they hurt. Though surrounded by courage as I knew I was, fear plagued me. I felt alone in the midst of horror. My heart stopped when the coach door opened and a bloody man, who was not one of the Earl's knights, thrust his arm into the carriage and grasped hold of my hand. I screamed, as shrilly as the spirit leaving me raised. The man's grip was unrelenting. I was pulled out of the still moving carriage so swiftly that I thought my arm would rip away from my body. But in the very instant before I hit the dirt road, I was hauled up by powerful arms and raised onto the back of a horse.

From the corner of my eye I could see the continued fighting, of both knights and men in plain clothes, on the road around us. I did not know how I would ever escape the turmoil. The horse upon which I had been raised broke into a gallop, then a swift run into the deep woods, past trees and thick brush that I feared would knock us down. Soon I could only faintly hear the clashes of swords far behind us. I closed my burning eyes in exhaustion.

***

When at long last our horse trod more slowly and I felt safe enough to loosen my clutch on my armored knight's waist, I took a deep breath as a soft breeze blessed my face. The sun was obscured by bountiful trees and yet we continued upon the same little-traveled path of our own design. The songs of birds serenaded our late afternoon journey, gratefully reminding me of the existence of hope. I found the peace and courage then to question my knight, "Sir?" I had wanted him to disclose his name and reassure me that we continued on our mission to meet with my betrothed. He reined our horse up, draped the reins over the mane and raised his helmet off his head, his dark hair moist with sweat and draping to his neck. My heart skipped a beat when he twisted and I met his piercing black eyes.

"Oh," I breathed, "Sir Lawrence…it is you."

He nodded but answered rather sadly, "It is now my mission alone to deliver you safely to the Earl." He appeared older to me now after the wear of battle, for the fine wrinkles beside his eyes were clearly evident. "My comrades are no doubt dead; we were barely able to escape ourselves." He turned away from me in that moment but I could see his devastation in his lowered head. My own feelings darted from confusion to fear, each emotion having a room of its own.

I peered ahead to notice a thatched cottage in a clearing of trees. It was small and the walls were dimly white, but there seemed to be no stir within it and I guessed it was abandoned. As we rode nearer I could see the birds that nested on the window's open shutters.. There was no turmoil that resided at this house, and surely Sir Lawrence would think it was a good place to rest from our travels for a short while.

"This is strange," he said, reining the horse up before the cottage door and dismounting, reaching up to take me into his arms and bring me down as well. But he did not release me and I could not help but to feel safe in his charge. He carried me, then my slippers brushed the leaves of a bush as he stopped at the door. I looked up to his face, noticing that his gaze was concentrated on the window rather than the door. He knocked on the wood with the end of his boot. I held my breath and watched the door.

In a moment's time the door cautiously creaked open, and an old man stood alone, his beard and his hair long and white. His face was stern though deeply wrinkled, but something in his light blue eyes was inviting. "A knight?" he questioned.

Sir Lawrence nodded. "That I am," he answered, "a knight who seeks shelter for a lady. Our caravan was attacked."

"By whom?" the old man questioned. "Robbers?"

"By the Welsh," answered Sir Lawrence, "who refuse to submit to Norman rule."

"I did not think they were this far into England," the old man said, then he took a step back "Come inside."

Sir Lawrence carried me into dim surroundings, following a stream of faint sunlight toward a table and chairs that the old man motioned toward. My knight sat me down into one of the chairs and released me, brushing my waist with his fingertips. My heart awoke with my mind.

"Is the Lady hurt?" the old man asked.

"No," Sir Lawrence answered as he wiped beads of sweat from his brow with his arm, "she is exhausted, and my comrades were killed."

The old man's drawn face appeared all the more shadowed with the wretched news. He grunted once, but I understood his unspoken consolation; he said, "I will pour some soup for supper."

"That is kind of you," I said, "thank you." The old man also reached for the bread beside the iron stove, unwrapping the napkin that had nestled it, then brought it to the table. Sir Lawrence sat down beside me without removing his sword, his dark eyes steadily fixed upon our host. His jaw was strong and his shoulders were wide, his chainmail armor and royal vest gently rising above his chest with each breath he took.

"What was the purpose of your mission?" the old man asked, his words sounding surprisingly tranquil.

Sir Lawrence grinned and the whole room seemed to come alive. "I cannot reveal that," he answered gently, "for this truth would surely endanger the Lady if she knew."

I watched him closely, for I was as curious as I knew the old man was. "Surely," I began, "you can tell our host more than that."

Sir Lawrence's soft smile disappeared. "You must not pursue this information, dear Lady, else you may not like what you find."

"What might she find?" questioned the old man, his silver eyebrows raised.

"Yes, what might I find?" I inquired, feeling more strength. "I would be pleased to know, Sir Lawrence."

My knight's coy grin returned as he answered, "You might find rebels, you might find artists, and you might find saints. Perfection is in the eye of the beholder. As for myself, I have freely chosen what God has chosen for me, and as far as I am able, I join faith with reason. I persevere that which I have uncovered along the journey because it intrigues me." He paused though I had wanted him to continue with his speech. Softly and with his gaze locked upon mine he said, "I drift too closely by what should remain secret." His eyes drew me beyond his words.

I brushed my forehead with my hand and asked, "Will you have mercy on me and tell me the reason that I am to be brought to my betrothed?"

Sir Lawrence grinned, his gaze never leaving mine. I had forgotten the old man who played our host on this shadowy evening, but the rough breath he drew reminded me. Sir Lawrence quickly offered, "My apologies, Sir, I am no doubt aware that this conversation has expressed little gratitude toward you for opening your home to us, and we are indeed grateful."

The old man merely nodded, and to my knight he said, "I think I will learn more about you and your lady if you forget that I am here."

My knight laughed, brushing his dark hair back with his hands. "Thank you, our humble host, for the bread and the rest."

The old man nodded once again and offered, "Sleep here tonight. You will be safe."

Sir Lawrence raised an eyebrow. I could feel his scrutiny of our old host. "We will accept your kind offer," he surprised me by saying, "and we are to leave at morning's first light."

"Good," the old man said, "It is done. Now, continue with your story."

Sir Lawrence leered toward our host and said, "No, I have said too much." I bit down on my bottom lip in anticipation of his next words.

"Do you think me a spy?" the old man questioned. "How was I to know that, in all the forest, as far away from the road as you are, you would find yourselves at my cottage? I do not have need for loyalty to country and king here, sir, but I do know travelers in need when I see them."

Sir Lawrence allowed the silence among them to linger for a moment, and then he conceded. "You are correct," he said. "I have questioned your generosity, and I offer my most sincere apologies."

"You were forgiven before you asked," the old man said. I watched his stern wrinkles grow softer in an instant. His blue eyes, strikingly clear, glanced to me before he stood from the table and walked into another room, from whence he emerged with a woolen blanket in his arms that he then rested upon the thatched floor.

With a gentle huff he said, "It will be dark soon, and there you are."

"Thank you," I said quickly.

In that moment Sir Lawrence's eyes grew kinder as he told the old man, "Someone may be sent to look in these woods when we do not reach our destination. My duty is to make Lady Meggy's welfare my first concern."

"Sir," the old man began to utter, but seemed to stumble with this sudden revelation of who I was. Then he resumed, "I was once a knight. I know how true your duty is."

"Her value is greater than the value of my own conscious," Sir Lawrence said with quiet conviction. Though I tried to remain unaffected, my heart swelled to bursting within my chest. I found just enough will and strength to hold my gaze upon him.

The old man cleared his voice and asked, "Is a Lady more important than a knight's honor?"

Sir Lawrence took a deep breath. "The weight of the world is on my shoulders, for I carry the safety of the Lady. The Earl of Pembroke himself asked it of me."

"I do not understand," I said meekly.

"There is great need of you," my knight began as he looked deeply into my eyes, "there is great need for what is within you and there is much at stake."

"I did not ask…" I tried to say.

"It is not for you to ask, my Lady, not for you to decide," he said. "It was the Earl's decision to call for you, and it was mine to save you. He glanced toward the window and the ever-darkening sky outside. "Come now," he said gently, "you shall get a sound night's rest before starting out tomorrow morning." He then stood from the table and walked toward the blanket on the floor, saying, "I will set aside a bed for you, my Lady." The old man passed through the doorway of the back room and disappeared out of sight completely.

Sir Lawrence spread the blanket out, then stood up straight and held a hand out toward me. "Come," he said, "you have nothing to fear here. I will be right outside the door." I did feel safe with him present, more protected than I could remember ever having felt. He touched the blanket again, saying, "Lie down." I did, and I allowed him to drape the blanket over me. Softly, he said, "There is more I want to tell you about all of this, but I cannot now."

"Sit beside me for another moment," I requested, peering into his dark eyes. He did so, but only after glancing toward his sword beside the table. Strands of black hair drifted before his eyes when he turned his gaze on me again. His new beard looked like a deep shadow upon his face as he rubbed his neck.

He sighed, then quietly said, "The Earl did not meet you by chance. You were orchestrated into his life, very carefully and very deliberately."

"How do you know this about me when I do not know it myself?" I asked.

"I have great interest in your life…and I have for a long while."

"Why? I do not understand."

"I have seen you at court in Canterbury, though you have not seen me. My Lady, I saw you before you met the Earl, before he was rewarded with an earlship. I saw you the day your father was killed in battle. I have been watching you ever since, in his stead you might say."

"Why did you not approach me? I would have been grateful."

"Because my only wish was for your well-being," he whispered. A chill crept through my skin. "It was I who suggested you for his bride." My mouth fell open, unbecoming of a lady I knew but I did not reproach myself. "His father was King William's cousin.

You will be forever safe with the Earl," he continued, "and I knew that. He needed your diligence for what is good and just. You see, he is descendant of a holy man."

"Is that the secret?" He winked at me, stopping my heart. But I said, "You have yet to explain his need for me now."

"I told you the truth when I told you that he was injured."

"How? Will he be well?"

"He was injured by a spy, whose identity we recently discovered. We do not want the traitor to learn of our plans, but somehow he did, given the battle we had with the Welsh. The spy is part of a sect of believers whose quest is for the British throne. They are willing to spill blood to see their cause through."

I was stunned and I could feel myself grasp his hand tightly. "The spy is Welsh?"

"No, he is not Welsh but he employs the Welsh." Then Sir Lawrence smiled, as coyly but peacefully as he had when I first met him. "I will let the Earl himself tell you more of that," he said. "For now, sleep," he said, gently releasing my hand, "and I will see you in the morning. Do not fear, for no one will pass through the doorway of this dwelling tonight."

***

I opened the heavy oak door of the cottage, met with the first dashes of light from the rising sun. I had expected to find my knight nearby but I caught no sight of him. My stomach tightened; I cautiously stepped outside the door and caught my breath with a sweet-smelling breeze.

"My Lady," Sir Lawrence walked briskly around the outside corner of the cottage and greeted me. He was not brandishing a smile this morning, and his eyes were filled with purpose and conviction. He walked past me toward our horse where he threw the blanket and saddle onto its back and fastened them. "We must leave this place."

"Where are we to go?"

"To the Earl, deeper into the forest," he said without looking at me. There existed a strange, unwanted distance between Sir Lawrence and myself this morning. I turned toward the cottage and started to walk inside.

"Where are you going?"

"I shall thank our host again before we leave," I answered, brushing the loose strands of my hair back.

He grabbed my arm rather firmly. "He has already gone," my knight told me, "before light."

My eyebrows narrowed and I glanced to his hand upon mine. "Is there need for urgency? I questioned.

He slowly released his grip as he said, "There is always need for urgency." He nodded and added, his dark eyes shining in the bold sunrise, "Come, get on," and he led me toward the powerful horse.

"I must get…" I had begun to say, but he raised me up onto the horse's saddled back without allowing me to finish, then carefully pulled himself on behind me. "Sir Lawrence, do you believe those men will find us here?"

"I am getting us away from this place before we find out," he answered.

We rode far away from the cottage, passing the same sort of trees we had upon finding ourselves there. I felt as jolted by the ride as I was by my fear of the unknown. The leaves of low branches brushed past my hair, the soft morning air tranquil to my lungs. Crackling branches and hard ground yielded an almost rhythmic sound as the pace of our horse slowed a bit. Water trickled somewhere nearby, though I could see no stream, and waking birds sang overhead as they so often dashed in flight from tree to tree.

I had not the resources to free my mind from this strange journey, and so inquired to my knight. "Sir

Lawrence," I began, tilting my head back so that he would hear me, "are they coming after us?"

He surprised me by laughing, moving me gently with the rise of his chest. "Of course they are," he said. "I will deliver you to the Earl though, I assure you of that. I would give my life for your safety."

"And your reputation?"

"Reputation is only relevant to the situation…"

Our silence then was disrupted by the songs of birds and the thuds of our horse's hooves upon solid ground. "What if the relevance is by nature," I questioned, "what then? Good reputation and a dedicated knight are identical, or they strive to be. One must compliment the other."

"Would you prefer I left you to the Welsh?"

"I glanced down to the armor that rest over his thigh. "I am glad you rescued me, Sir Lawrence. I would never want you to think that I am ungrateful."

"Then it is settled," he said, gazing steadily into my eyes. "It is settled and I have found you as God intended I find you." He paused and grinned subtly. "I watched the stars one night," he said, "and they spelled out your name. Their brightness attested to the signature of God."

"You did not submit as readily as you suggest," I mustered.

"You are the world at my fingertips, and the world must turn slowly."

I felt a shudder in my heart. My mind was clouded by a tunnel of clarity. "You speak words, when it is I who am uncertain of you," I revealed. "The truth is turned 'round, for you are grounded and I am floating." I abruptly lowered my head and sat away from him. I knew I had said too much. He was no longer a knight of my betrothed's choosing, for he was chosen of God and his grandeur extended beyond life. His words gave him wings, and to be in the presence of such greatness terrified me.

He nudged the horse into a quicker pace. His arms were still around me as he grasped the reins loosely. He seemed to sense my limpness and held me tighter, but peace was to be elusive. I stared to the forest ahead when I heard the thunder of horses swiftly approach us. "Hold on tight," Sir Lawrence quietly commanded me, and I did so. I felt no fear from him, as he began to lead our horse out of the road without a sound.

But a cluster of horses and their riders emerged from the dense trees, their dark cloaks keeping their identity a secret. Yet, my knight remained calm. The riders reined up directly in front of us. The man in the lead drew the hood of his cloak back, revealing a hardened, middle-aged face and sandy blond hair. Suddenly he smiled, and I felt a jolt of laughter from Sir Lawrence as he held me.

"Sir Richard," my knight began, "what brings you into the woods, dressed like a monk, no less."

"You are a sight worth seeing," Sir Richard exclaimed. "I had thought you were killed on the road to Pembroke with the others."

There was a noteworthy pause before Sir Lawrence answered, "No, my mission was to keep the Lady safe, and we escaped." His voice, however, was filled with a sort of haunting that made me cringe. In the silence afterward I wondered if his words were to become his prison.

"You were very blessed," acknowledged Sir Richard, "for only one man rode free of the Welsh, besides you, and that man describes numbers severely uneven. The Earl's knights never had a chance. We lost some of our most loyal and humble servants on that day."

I felt Sir Lawrence's discomfort in the very tension of his arms about me. "It was my failing not to have died among them," he said, "but my duty, as I promised the Earl, was to keep the Lady safe."

"I know," Sir Richard said, "and he waits in the Priory outside the wall of Pembroke castle."

"Does he know that Lady Meggy is safe?"

Sir Richard nodded. "He will soon hear."

"Then we shall go," my knight said with conviction, and abruptly prompted our horse forth on route to join my betrothed again.

"You did not ask if the Earl is well," I told him over the wind.

The silence that often accompanied my knight, overtook him. For many strides of our horse, he did not answer me. Leaves brushed my cheek, a shadowed chill caused me to shiver. I had not the will to repeat my question, and gratefully, Sir Lawrence at last answered without being provoked. His voice was low and sorrowful as he said, "The Earl's duty has left him ill at heart. He searches for a replacement, for if his wounds overtake him and he wishes to be prepared. God's hands rest upon him, I am only his servant."

"If his wound does not heal…" I repeated with great fear in my tone.

"Do not be anxious," Sir Lawrence said over the wind but quickly seemed to shift into a daze.

I tried to startle him out of it by asking, "How seriously is he wounded? Tell me truthfully."

His low voice rattled the air about me when he answered, "That would be impossible. You would not know from whence it came and to where it will go. It would fill you, and then overwhelm you. Your mind would overflow with understanding until you perish in a flood of disbelief and uncertainty. No one is prepared to know the depth within guarded secrets such as these. The knowledge must be slowly and steadily revealed to you, like a gentle, soaking rain."

I bit down on my lip and narrowed my eyebrows, and thought for a moment longer. "Is this how I am to learn my purpose for my betrothed? And if his lordship is taken from him, then I too must leave England."

My knight laughed. "You, my Lady, know not your high value."

I shook my head though, because I was not satisfied with his answer. I had to insist, "Sir Lawrence, please answer me, for I *must* know my fate."

"None of us knows our fate. I do not think that was the Earl's intention."

"Then what are the Earl's intentions?"

"You know as well as I do, my Lady," he proclaimed. "It is a matter of listening. Would you listen, truly listen, as your duty is revealed…that is to say, your 'sacred duty'? Will you be ready to ride through the clouds like Abraham and Ezekiel did?"

"What do I have to do with the likeness of Abraham?"

"He was God's chosen friend," Sir Lawrence said, his armor shifting with the shrug of his shoulders. "Am I talking in circles, my Lady?"

"Why have I not seen or heard of you before yesterday, though I know what you have said?" I asked. "If you are a knight in the Earl's charge, surely I would have known your name."

"Not always," he asserted. "It was his lordship's will that my identity remained a secret from you until the day of his replacement."

"You are confusing me again."

"Perhaps," he began lightly, reining our horse around cluster after cluster of trees. "Soon, we will join together what Man in all His fear has separated. You will know that nothing can lure you away from your destiny."

"Stop!" I blurted. Strands of my golden hair flew

on the breeze beside my eyes, and I looked away. "Truly, I cannot grasp this."

But he laughed again, blurting "You overfloweth, my Lady, for you have the answers you seek and you do not know it." He was silent for a moment then, but questioned himself aloud, "What is a castle doing here in the middle of a forest?"

"What?" I asked.

"Look there," he directed, pointing well beyond our immediate surroundings, deep into the mysteries of the forest, "through the trees…there." My attention peaked, I peered ahead into a thick growth of trees…and a grey structure behind them.

"Yes, I see it," I said faintly. Sir Lawrence reined our horse nearer to the structure, and in time I recognized that the structure was a castle, and that the castle bore no attempt of military defense. It seemed as open as the most humble of country houses, waiting to become the weary traveler's answered prayer. My uncertainty was overcome by my intrigue, for I was fascinated by the beauty, the boldness, and the strangeness of the magnificent castle.

Evening soon began to shadow the forest, which may have been what prompted Sir Lawrence to rein our horse toward the *open* castle gates and halt. "Someone might await us," I whispered into my knight's ear. He said nothing. "I am frightened."

"There is no need to be," he tried to reassure me.

"We do not know what lies ahead."

"That is true," he said. He nudged our mount forth into a slow gait. I dared not speak, for the horse's hooves echoed loudly upon stone amidst this tall fortress. "Come," he told me quietly, reining our horse to a halt, "we will rest the horse and see ourselves what surrounds us." I did not disagree, and Sir Lawrence dismounted and helped me down, then tied our horse up on a rack several strides into the gate.

He took my arm securely into his and we walked across the ground, then we found ourselves standing before a single great, dark door. Sir Lawrence clicked down the heavy iron knocker. I bit my lip and held onto his arm more tightly. He stood solidly beside me, his chainmail armor dulled with the onset of the evening hours.

The great door then budged; my fingernails scratched against my knight's armor. An old man stood alone as the door creaked open. I turned to Sir Lawrence, my eyes wide with shock, my mouth ajar. My knight stared at the old man and drew his dagger from the brace at his waist. "What are you doing here? You have deceived us. Do you not abide in the cottage we stayed at last night?" he questioned.

The old man, the same white-bearded man whom had opened his dwelling to us, stretched his hand out toward us now. "Come inside," he invited. "As it was at the cottage, so shall it be here. I am the servant of Lord Arnulf's servant."

"Why are you here?" Sir Lawrence questioned again, this time standing firm until he received an answer.

"Because this is my true home. I am King of the Forest. One can never tell what is hidden without the outward appearance."

"How can you be King? You are disillusioned."

The old man grinned. "You are not the first to ask that question," he said. "Come inside, and you will begin to know the answers."

"Where were you this morning?" Sir Lawrence asked before following the old man's lead into the castle.

"The rise of the sun calls me here."

"The rise of the sun called me away from your cottage as well, therefore you left *before* the rise of the sun."

The old man's leer, though determined, was also gentle. Something about him, maybe the very softness in his light eyes, led me to trust him. "I do not conceal anything from you, Sir Lawrence," he assured, "inwardly nor outwardly. My deception has been sought after by you, but that you will not find."

My knight's stare did not fall away from the old man until another moment of studied silence passed. "We will follow you," my knight relinquished, "but only because I see no cowardice in your eyes."

The old man nodded. "And so it is," he said. "Follow me," he added, and so we did. Coolness rushed me as the dimness nearly enveloped us a few steps beyond the door. The old man raised a blazing torch from a bracket in the stone wall; the sound of flames echoed.

"What is the purpose of your castle?" Sir Lawrence questioned.

The old man took another step, then stopped and turned toward us. "As I have told you," he answered, "I am King, and a king rules his land. A good king rules with justice and integrity, as I have thus intended."

"How long has this castle been here? I have never seen it before, and I have been through this forest."

"It has been here since there has been a need," the old man answered with keen sincerity.

"What is the need?" questioned my knight. In the dancing shadows I thought I saw his jaw clinch as though he stood in preparation of the most unissued answer. I quietly took a deep breath, for I too felt that I must brace myself.

The old man shifted the torch from his left hand to his right. "Your question breeds the answer, so ask only that which you are certain you want to know. Everyone wants to know the answers eventually, but it is a matter of asking the right questions. Different questions will lead you through different mazes. Be sure that the one you take is the one you intend to take."

"I am armed for the question as well as for the answer," promised Sir Lawrence.

"Then come with me," the old man said. We resumed his previous journey through the castle hallway. "To whence do you intend to find yourself when it is all over?"

"Why do you ask me that?"

"Once I know your destination, I can show you which door to pass through."

"Is the end known before the beginning and the middle?"

"Indeed it is," the old man answered, shooting a poignant glance our way. "The middle of the journey proves your endurance to God. But first, you must begin."

"I *have* begun," Sir Lawrence assured. "I seek the Earl."

"Yet, you have found the King," proclaimed the old man.

"So you have said, but the Earl that I seek will set me on the proper course to reach answers once only revealed to the ancients."

The old man cornered a slight grin, and then glanced at me. "What do you think he will tell you? I tell you that I come only to the most worthy."

"My betrothed, the Earl of Pembroke, will tell us his intent," I answered quickly. The aged Forest King took a few more steps then turned back, toward us, the torch flame casting a mysterious glow upon his face. "Sir," I began, hesitating, "it is my guess that you have lured us here, to this castle, on purpose, though I do not know what for. My betrothed is not with us, we have not yet seen him. Tell us, Sir, what is your reason?"

"My reason," the old man answered, "is the same as I have for living in a cottage when I am King of the Forest. I live for the middle. My joy is there, for my joy is in enrichment, not of possessions, but of my true self. You, my dear ones, must find your true selves, and the only way you can do this is by residing in the middle. Fight, in the joy of the middle, and God will reveal to you the nature of your true selves as though you have gazed into His very eyes. Then, you can count yourselves lucky and blessed. Only then will you be ready to move onto the destination."

I said nothing though I lowered my gaze. My knight took up my cause for me, saying, "We seek the Earl of Pembroke to gain direction from him, whatever that may be."

"The lady we seek is Lord Arnulf's betrothed He may tell you where to go next, but she will remain by his side once arrived. You must take account of your possessions."

"People are not possessions." I said.

"People are free," the old man acknowledged, "though ideas tend to find themselves entrapped." He smiled, continuing, "It is getting late, dear guests. I will show you to your rooms, where you may sleep for the night. If you chose to continue on your former journey in the morning, you are free to do so."

Sir Lawrence nodded, and I refused to release his arm throughout the musty-smelling cold castle, up the steep stairway, and toward my room, where I parted from my two escorts to go inside.

***

I awoke in a strange bed, doused in the moonlight that streamed in through my bare window. I turned my head and held my breath, for Sir Lawrence sat on the rug upon the floor beside my bed, leaning against the stone wall. His eyes became fixed on mine the moment I looked toward him.

"Why are you in my room?" I asked, pulling my warm woolen blanket up to my chin.

He smiled, which eased my heart. "I have come," he said, "so that you might be safe."

"Your presence is the reason that I am," I answered too swiftly for thought.

He smiled. His eyes warmed my blood. "The night is almost half gone," he told me, "and we still need to discuss where we are going tomorrow."

"I thought you knew that."

"I do, though I know not what you are willing to endure. It means the difference between the long route and the short route." He leaned forward, away from the wall, his gaze still focused on mine. "The long route may separate us, though it will allow us to reach Lord Arnulf. The short route would not separate us."

"We would not be separated on the short route? Is it easier?"

"Yes," Sir Lawrence answered, "and for that reason we will be together."

I lowered my head and pondered for a moment, looking into his eyes and saying, "Sir Lawrence, we must learn the answers we seek, simply because the questions themselves are not clear."

He nodded, lowering his head for the first time since I awoke to find him in my room. "The long route will have the answers, because we will not be together when we see them." I knew what he meant, for I was almost as distracted by him now as he was by me. "We must leave now, at this moment, before our old host wakes up," he said. Slowly, he got up and turned away toward the door of my room. "I will wait for you outside," he said, "you can decide which route we take but we must quickly leave this castle."

***

The wind of a stormy early morning caught me as soon as I stepped out of the castle with my knight, disheveling my hair after I had braided it. I clung to my dress. The sky was dark gray with no hint of sun, and the trees were as windswept as the dress I tried to hold still.

My knight tugged me toward the gates. Dark ravens swooped down in front of our faces with unbelievable speed. Claps of thunder startled me; pelting rain was relentless; branches shot to the ground. My face must have reflected the terror I felt, for Sir Lawrence took me to his armor and held me tightly.

"Our horse! It's gone!" I screamed over the powerful gusts of wind. "How do we leave?" I was frightened.

"You do not leave," boomed a familiar voice behind us. Both my knight and I spun around. "You will now embark on a journey," the King of the Forest revealed, his hair weighted even longer with rain water, "though not measured in steps taken. The distance you will cross will be the distance in your mind."

"You cannot force us to stay," Sir Lawrence yelled over the wind.

"No truer words have ever been spoken, for I am an old man and you are young and strong. My army is my faith in God."

My knight squinted; I pushed wet strands of my hair away from my face. He asked, "Why do you want to keep us here?"

"I do not; I want you to find your own way out. However, you must be armored by character, and *that* you may only acquire as you seek a way out."

I glanced to my knight, whose mouth was open, rain water dripping from his lips. "You cannot do this. Lord Arnulf awaits our arrival. He will send his men when his betrothed fails to meet him."

"There are not many knights remaining," the old King said, "and you are ridden with guilt because you are one of those who remain."

"The character I acquire will be by my own choosing – not yours," Sir Lawrence said with conviction.

The old man grinned. "Character is in the heart, not the decision. I will help you find your heart…come with me now. There is no way to leave, except on foot, and the storm itself may kill you before it is over."

My knight began to shake his head in refusal, but with the chilling rain drenching my dress, I could only stare to him, my eyes pleading. His gaze filled me with peace, even if our intention came to pass, even for the will of God, even for the will of this elderly King, even by distance.

"We will stay," Sir Lawrence shouted without looking away from me.

"You have chosen wisely," the King of the Forest commended. "Let us get out of this storm."

***

I gazed to my knight for comfort. We were warm now, for we stood near a fire in the great dining hall of the castle, and we had changed into dry clothes which were much like the clothes we had worn before. My knight was without his armor at present, though his dagger was fixed to his thigh, and his clothes draped loosely over his body. His dark hair was still damp and reached past his ears, and his black eyes were ever keen. He broke a small loaf of bread he had gotten from the table and gave me half.

"This place appears to be a castle on the outside…" the old man said as he walked into the room, "but you have entered into a maze." He stared to Sir Lawrence and continued, "Now you will see what it is like to be in your own mind. Tell me what you find, and be sure to ask the right questions. You cannot find the door unless you ask the right questions."

Sir Lawrence stood from his chair. "We are to be held prisoner here, then," he seethed.

The old man's eyebrows raised as he held one finger into the air. "Ahh…" he began, "you came back on your own free will."

"What right do you have to do this?"

"A King's right, and the right of a father who loves his son." Sir Lawrence's eyebrows narrowed. I thought he might be angered by the provoked confusion. "As God is the Father of All," the King said, "I am the Father of the Forest and everything in it – and now you are in it. My Son, even in my love for you, I do not do this. You have asked for this yourself when you returned. Your heart is eager for challenge, for it will become stronger and deeper as well. What you see will be your level. Let your heart guide you."

"Where to?"

I rest my bread onto the table. "No need to fear," I whispered to Sir Lawrence, "as you saved me, you can now save yourself."

"How long have you been betrothed to Lord Arnulf?" the old man asked me.

I lowered my head, for I was reminded of a world beyond this forest, a world I had previously belonged to. "Not long," I answered.

"Do you know yourself…before you marry him? Do you doubt the betrothal? Is your heart made of stone, or fire?" he questioned.

I raised my gaze. "My heart is composed of the memories that dwell there," I answered honestly.

The old man nodded. "I understand." Then, he turned, saying, "May God be with you," and walked out of the dining hall. The stone walls suddenly appeared darker and seemed colder.

I looked toward Sir Lawrence; he looked to me; and neither of us said a word. To me, the air around us watched with peculiar interest, as if to see what our next action would be. Then, I understood. "Our justice will be the measure of our actions," I breathed.

My knight nodded. "Action gives birth to character…one must 'do' before one can 'become.' We must keep searching," he said, "not only for a way out but for the principles of that way out, and for reasons deeper than what we can clearly see."

The old man nudged the great door open and popped his head inside for a brief moment. " I forgot to tell you," he announced, "that because there are different reasons for your being here, you must set forth onto different paths. The Lady will leave through the far door," he pointed to the opposite end of the hall, "and you, Sir Lawrence, will leave through this one, after me." My knight and I glanced toward one another in silence. We were as stunned as we had been the moment we came back into the castle out of the storm, rain, wind, and thunder that still plundered the forest outside. There was no escaping the echo and power of the thunder against these castle walls.

"We need not do as he says," my knight tried to reassure me, "you may leave through the same door as I. It makes no difference."

But courage flowed through me and became me, for I knew that there was indeed a need for the separation. "No," I answered with great conviction, "we must do as the King of the Forest has prescribed. In that way, I know we have to find the answers we seek. And I especially have so many questions that mean nothing without answers. Questions will bring me no nearer to the mystery that surrounds my betrothed, but only duty will lead my heart to water and quench me. Please understand. Whatever I must endure to find answers, I will endure it."

He grinned. "You are brave."

"I am diligent."

He nodded. "How will I know that you are safe?" he asked, raising his gentle gaze that I held with my own.

"I will find a way to tell you, like you will find a way to hear me. No matter where we are, whether space separates us or thought does, you will always know."

Sir Lawrence stared into my eyes and nodded. "Then we begin," he breathed. "If you think you are in danger, my Lady, I will find you no matter where you are."

My smile was weak and my eyes welled with tears. "I must find answers on my own, without any help…" I whispered through my sorrow.

"I know." He held my chin up with his fingers and winked, then stood aside as I rushed past him and bolted through the door.

***

As I stood on the other side of the door I took a deep breath to regain my sense of self and time. The room into which I had entered was much colder than the dining hall, and darker as well. As I rubbed my arms for warmth and squinted to see, I felt the stark, painful truth…I was utterly alone. My heart more than ached…it slowly tore in two. My stomach felt pitted and empty, my mind confused and terrified.

After an instant I notice that the door opposite from where I stood was slightly ajar. I reached with one finger and pushed it open further, but I could not see…not without stepping within.

Wind rushed my face; the door slammed shut behind me. I was surrounded by darkness, and I was alone. The silence became a shrill noise of torture and immeasurable pain. And I was alone. Even in a crowd, I would be alone. I was without my protecting knight, my knight who would save me before he saved himself. Sadness and mourning engulfed me.

***

I waited, shivering beside the window, longing to jump. I wondered if I had made the right choice. The screams were all around me, screams that had begun as faint the moment I passed through the door, screams from crowds of unseen people; their voices blood-curdling. My mind though, wrung deeper, for I had never before longed so much to be safe. I longed to feel the touch of my savior's hand upon mine, to feel embraced by his gaze.

"You are thinking of your betrothed," announced a starkly unkind voice.

I whirled around, though I could not see through the darkness. "Who is there?" I cried. "Tell me!" But no one spoke. There were still more shrill screams.

I stepped to the ledge of the window and peered out, though I could see nothing but the faint outline of the window sill itself. There was no way for me to see how far down the ground was.

I held my hands over my ears in an effort to silence the screams, but they were still too loud. Suddenly something sharp – the fingernails of a hand – grasped my shoulder. Without a thought I leapt through the window.

Moment upon moment of plummeting and flashes of light passing beside me. I had been higher than I thought, but I was not afraid. The wind forced such pressure upon me that my hands went numb. Coldness cut through me like a knife. At last my fall ended with my breath knocked out of me – I had landed on something soft, though when I felt to both sides there was only rocky ground.

My surroundings became clearer as my breath grew steadier. My jaw lowered, for even these dim images were not those of the forest. Instead, I recognized the bed in my room, raised off the floor but draped in a bedspread as dark as the night. I stood with weakened legs upon rocky ground, my feet cold and bruised.

Though I squinted and strained to see, shadows blended into darkness.

My eyes were drawn to a glisten above the outline of the bed, and I could see dim reflections in a tall, wide mirror and a flaming candle fixed to its frame. I inched closer, climbing upon the bed again in an effort to see my own reflection. I reached toward it in disbelief, for my face was drawn and distorted, and my hair was knotted and laden with mud. My eyes were as empty as the night that surrounded me. For a moment I thought that something was wrong with the mirror itself but the image looking back was indeed my own. I squeezed my eyes closed and pressed on the sides of my head with all my strength. Then it was that the truth confronted me – I could not remember why I was here, nor how I had arrived. Fear plunged through my breath and stabbed my heart, leaving me paralyzed. I glanced to the mirror again, repulsed. My hands shook and my knees trembled. I stood up, off the bed, and staggered with a hunger in my stomach that made me feel like I had not eaten in weeks. But contentment of a full stomach would not be meant for one as hideously obscured as the mirror had shown me to be.

"You are wicked, you are wicked, you are wicked," chanted three women, ugly though they seemed not to know it by the finery they wore. "You can do no good!" one of them squawked. "You are nothing, while we…" they said with a self-delighted wave of their hands and dance in their feet, "are all that is good in the world."

My lips shook and tears streaked my dirty, hideous face. "Go away!" I cried.

"It is not for you to desire," said the elder and the biggest of the women. "You deserve the worst of everything and you will pay in your own misery."

"Pay for what?" I asked.

"For everything you have ever received in your life that we have not. You are in our world now," she hissed, "and you will have only what we give you." I cried harder, but they pressed on, "Do not weep. Your tears are only those of a selfish fool, a selfish, blubbering fool."

I shook, my fingernails digging into the flesh of my face. I so desperately wanted to run past them but they said that I could not, and I knew I would not remember where to go if I did gain the courage.

"You can never leave this place!" the youngest of the hags bellowed.

I bit down on my lip and sobbed. They said more, though I could only hear vague murmurs. I turned toward the mirror again, my dress was tattered rags and bore no hint of color. In fact, as I looked around, even the shadows had become nothingness. It was as though the life had been drained from all that had once possessed life. My head spun. In the mirror, my reflection had grown to be as wide as the biggest of the horrid witches. I did not know myself anymore; my face was doused with my own tears.

"Stay here and see how ugly you are," the witches said together, "we are beautiful and we live in beauty." Their giggles and laughter wrung at my stomach. I could no longer breathe; I gasped for air. The three women disappeared from my sight in a flash and I fell onto the jagged rock at my feet and took the most desperate breath that I could imagine. The faint candlelight beside the mirror flickered out and I was in blackness once again. I cried...

In another moment the mirror had disappeared with the hags but I could feel how repulsive I had become with my hands. I ventured into the darkness, groping to the rocks to find a path. Carefully, I stepped one bare foot before the other; I felt only darkness and pain. Soon the pain caused by the rocks prevented me from moving, unbearable as it was, and equal to the wrenching pain in my heart. Emptiness seemed to devour me, feeding my own hunger with the emptiness of myself. I touched my lips, trembling with my sobs, and felt more than my own tears from them. Surely it was my blood I felt. My pain was numbing, but I forced myself on with sheer will.

"Lady Meggy, come over here," a deep, plummeting voice beckoned. I looked up, and though I could see nothing I stood and stepped forward in the direction of the voice, for I desperately needed help.

"Why did you call me that?" I asked.

However the speaker did not acknowledge my question. Instead, he repeated with great power in his deep voice, "Come over here."

"I am coming," I said obediently.

"Faster," said the voice, unfamiliar and demanding.

"I cannot find you in the dark," I cried. Truly, I was terrified that the speaker would be angered by my lack of competence.

Indeed, he was. "Right here!" he shouted and then grabbed my arm through the dark. "Here! Are you blind? If it is too dark for you to see it is your own fault. If you had listened to the three beautiful women by the mirror you would know where you stand."

I nodded and lowered my head. "I know," I succumbed.

"Then you know something," the voice said. "Now turn and go back up the stairway, return to the mirror and those three beautiful women again and ask them for guidance."

My arm was released by him but it throbbed with the pain left by his tight grip. "I will go," I said. My head lowered, I tried to find the stairway he had spoken of. I tripped up the first step, and lowered myself down to employ my painful hands on the journey as well. I groped and struggled, climbing one step at a time. But I was overwhelmed, completely overwhelmed with the thought that I would never reach the top and I knew that. Even if I did, the three hags would be awaiting me to torture my soul.

"My Lady," said a different voice, wonderful and fearless. My heart stopped, though not with fear but with sudden amazement. "I am the love of your heart," he said gently.

"Love of my heart?" I pleaded, fearful that I would disappoint him with my lack of understanding. My skin burned with my desire to hear more from him.

I almost fainted with the vibration of his voice through my blood; his lips softly brushed my ear as he said, "I am dead to you." He kissed my neck though, so tenderly and with such purpose and meaning. "In order to reach me you must gain the sight of light and truth."

"I will do anything for you, for you have shown me kindness."

"If you would…" he whispered, stroking my face with his hand, hot tears of gratitude streaming from my eyes; all there was in the world now was love regardless of my surroundings. The blessed man continued to run his fingertips over my neck, to trace my lips with his. I wanted only his love.

"Please, my love," I whispered, "tell me your name. Why are you patient with me? Especially if I have forgotten about your great and merciful love? Why do you love me like this? How can I be worthy of you, as ugly as I am?"

"You saw yourself as the witches wanted you to see yourself, for you are beautiful and they know they are ugly, and they must renounce you to build themselves up. But a castle cannot be built on rubble, for it will always fall and the truth of its foundation will be known."

My heart ached with love, as though love was born inside my chest. "Please," I breathed, "do not ever leave me."

"Why would you say that?" he asked me with his kiss and embrace. "Why do you fear that I would leave you?" I began to shake my head but I could not answer, for I truly did not know. "Who has left you before? Who has loved you as I love you?" His voice was still soft and peaceful.

"I am frightened," I began, feeling the strong need for truth in his presence. "I am terrified that I will be taken away from you."

"That is not possible, not when your love is so strong that you would die for it. The only way that we would ever be separated is if you yourself willed it."

"No," I briskly disagreed, "that could never happen."

"It matters only that you remember your love for me, so that you will not survive in your fear of love's death."

"Is that why you told me that you were dead to me? Am I so bound by my fear of being separated from you that I cannot see the path that will bind us? In the light, where you dwell? Just to be near you…" my voice diminished into a whisper, "I live to be near you."

His warm, tender lips pressed against my forehead. I could no longer feel my pain. I was breathless with his beauty that I could not see. He barely pulled back to say, "Live for me, and I will find you again. Keep going forward, and live for the hope of me."

"I will," I answered, tears of hope raining through my very existence.

***

When I opened my eyes again I realized that I lay in the comfort of my own bed in the Forest King's castle. I was safe and I could see all that surrounded me, the large bed in which I lay, the golden-hued dress that was draped over the end of it, and the clear, tall mirror that stood against the wall at the end of my bed. As I moved toward it I realized it reflected me now as I was used to seeing myself, my long golden color hair streaming over my shoulders, my frame gentle and capable beneath my white nightdress...though I wondered how I now wore a nightdress. Regardless, whatever I had to face now, no matter what lay ahead of me, I could face it because I knew I had a great love.

I pushed the blankets off of me and stood out of bed. The rug over the floor was as warm as I had remembered, against my feet that had neither cuts nor sores. I grinned to myself, for my memory was clear and I felt as though I gained myself again. When the beautiful secret man brought me love, he re-instated my memory.

Slowly, I stepped toward the door. Rays of sunlight showed me my way, glistening upon the brass lion-headed door knob that I grasped. When I creaked the door open, a dread suddenly entered my flesh for a lonely void awaited me outside in place of what should have been a long hall. I could sense a floor at my feet still, but I could see nothing.

"You cannot leave this room!" I fell back with the terrible shrieking voice – I could not distinguish at first if it belonged to a man or woman. Tears heated my face at once, and I knew again that I was detested and revolted. I felt as ugly as I had when I looked in the mirror last night. I lost my sense of time, as soon as I stepped out of the room. Again, I heard the hags' horrible laughter – being confined to the bedroom had been a blessing. "You will learn nothing outside your room, you will know only what your hands can reach to," said the oldest, biggest hag who I could now see before me. "You are living what you *are!*"

Trembles of sorrow again restrained me. "Leave me," I weakly muttered, aware of the wrath that would befall me for speaking at all.

"Silence!" the younger witch shouted. "You were born of nothing and you return to nothing!"

"How can I escape this horror if I cannot leave this room?"I cried.

The hags' evil laugh made me shrink in my own skin. "You are not worthy of escape!" the old hag said. I stepped back and turned into my room, then sat on the bed where I lowered my face into my hands and shook my sobs. "You are not even worthy of our presence. But here we are, so indeed you must always be grateful to us. You will worship us." The deadness in my heart, the void in my stomach, the sadness of my mind, were all things that I would adapt to with time. I could not wish for something more, I knew that now.

Then the evil man who had taunted me after my fall last night appeared beside me in my room and spoke to me with a voice that cringed my soul. "Never fear," he said, "we are all you will ever have and we will never leave you." I shook, but I knew not to cry harder or my surroundings would grow even bleaker. But amidst their wild laughter at me, they left and slammed the door with great force. I stood up from the bed and looked around, my surroundings had quickly grown so much darker. My heart was too broken to feel anything; my soul was too powerless to believe in its own existence.

Then I took a deep breath that replenished me, so I lay down on the bed again, though engulfed by darkness. I wanted my freedom. I longed to escape, but even stronger was my longing to be loved by the beautiful man who had saved me last night. I longed for his soft but assured voice, for his gentle but protective touch, for his ever beautiful and intriguing being. Where was he now…now that I needed him desperately again? I longed to be comforted by the sight of him. I wanted to find him.

"Meggy…" a beautifully deep voice, full of love, called.

I melted. "My love," I whispered.

"Have you forgotten the hope in me?"

"No!" I cried with tears of conviction. "I will never forget you."

He touched my face with warm fingertips. "Though you may forget the hope of me. Hope, my love, is truth, and you have been blinded to the truth."

"It is true that I cannot see you…everything is so dark and filled with shadows."

"You see what you have accepted," he said, "but you are more than you know. Live and breathe that."

"I will live by every word you say, "I told him.

"Then show me," the beautiful man said. "And call me by my name. You give me the world when I hear my name in your voice."

"Jesus…" I breathed, "Tell me what to do so I can leave this nightmare and live with you?"

"Do not think of yourself."

"I can think only of you, my love."

"As I can think only of you," Jesus said. "You live in darkness because you think you are not loved – but I love you, Meggy. I love you so much that I created the world and everything in it for you. I am your light. My passion is for you."

I closed my eyes to listen to his words as though they were soft raindrops falling upon my parched sin. "I love you -" I breathed, "though I do not understand why you call me *your* love."

"Because you are," he answered with more love than I knew possible. "You are my bride, the love of my life. You are my breath, and my life. You must allow me to be yours."

"I do allow it!"

"I will be always, then. It is me that you have sought."

I was confused though; my eyebrows narrowed. "I know you?"

Jesus laughed, a charming, vivacious laugh. "No, no hint has ever been given to you about me, for if you knew, I would be your light and you would not live in darkness. They would not deceive you as they do."

"How do they deceive me?"

"By trapping you in a narrow mind when you are so much more. They themselves could not be more if you were not less. In the smallness there is only darkness, but as you learn, the more your mind will stretch and you will begin to see light, and you will watch that light grow."

"What must I do?"

"You must not do," he breathed into my ear, "you must *be*. Be in love with me and your heart will have life once again."

I shook my head and touched the side of his face though I could not see him. "I care nothing for what may be opened up to me," I promised. "I care only for loving you. I can live here, with these people, forever, if I am aware and full of love for you."

"You are love beyond love," he said. "You are the world at my fingertips, and you are worthy of me."

I cried and fell into his arms. "How do you know me so well?"

"I knew you before you knew yourself."

"Who am I? Besides my name, who am I, in truth?" He drew my hands to his lips and kissed them. "Am I not who those people want me to be? I form to their wishes."

Then, his voice became like thunder when he said, "You *are* love."

"I am love?"

"*You are love*. I have given you your identity, now cling to it." He then held my hand tightly in his and led me to the door. "I want to show you something," he said softly into my ear.

"Those witches told me that I could not leave," I said. "What if they are near?"

But my Jesus' laugh was gentle and confident. "They cannot stand in the way of true love, for love is stronger than iron. If you were clad in locks and chains, Meggy, my love would free you. And hear – I said not '*I would free you*' but '*my love would free you*.' Where I am weak, love makes strong. Though you may fear, though you may be faithless, love is unaware of fear and endeavors to release you of the bondage of a small mind. Now come, Love."

I made myself pliable to his touch, and I did go with him when he opened the door and led me out of the room.

Once again, darkness prevailed through the castle as in my bedroom, though once led outside the castle itself, I was taken aback by the beauty and tranquility of moonlight. My mouth slightly ajar, I stared to the lake that this beautiful man had brought me to, and watched glowing moonbeams caressing the waters in amazement.

I quickly turned, suddenly hopeful of seeing my beautiful Jesus' face, however sadness overcame me when I realized that his face was still too shadowed to be seen. "Do not be sorrowful, Meggy, for you see me in your heart. Look at the light you have already brought into the darkness with your love."

I glanced to the glowing moonlight. "I did this?"

"Your creation," he simply answered.

"Oh, my beautiful Jesus, what can I do with it?"

"You can learn, and through your learning this light will grow brighter. In the light, you will see the path to freedom that has been there all along."

"Are you there, in the freedom? Will I be able to see you?"

"I will always be where you are, whether you see me or not. You are my home. Your love is my kingdom."

"Let me go with you now!" I pleaded, and flung myself at his feet.

He fell to his knees and clung to me as firmly as I clung to him. "No matter how much I want you to come to me now, you cannot. I will not think of myself, I will only think of you and your illumination if you stay and learn. The more you learn, the nearer to me you will become."

"But it will take longer."

"I know," he agreed tenderly, "but you will never remember me completely any other way."

"What?" I asked, very confused.

"The truth is in the light, and the light is in learning. Meggy, memory is the light itself. The more you learn, the more light you will shed on the truth of who I am to you."

"What brought you to speak to me?"

"You needed to fall in love with me, without fear. You need to be willing to live and find the light that will come through me. You are bathed in love, and the water will awaken you to the truth. You would not feel love or gain the light to see truth unless you had been engulfed by darkness."

"What is the darkness made of, if the light is memory?" I asked.

"The darkness is your sorrow. It is the lie, and it is *not* knowing. It is deception. Not remembering truth announces the presence of manipulation."

I took a deep breath and looked to the glistening water. A slight ripple emulated near the shore nearest to me, then the ripple grew into a soft wave, pleasant and safe. Oddly, it did not move anywhere, but it grew toward the sky without shifting right nor left, front nor back.

The song that graced my ears was perfect in every way, for the instrument that gave it life was the water itself. I could see by the way the wave swelled and how delicate the fringe of white streamed from the ripple, how intricate and needed each drop was to the crest of wave in this moonlit world.

"The lake is showing you," my Jesus explained, "the beauty of its song is like the truth that will prevail from your confusion. This fountain has been brought before you in love, for it knows that you will release it from these shadows. The light you will bring is not only for your freedom, but it will bring freedom to the world that surrounds you."

"I bring freedom to more than myself if I learn about the world in which I live?"

"Yes," my beautiful Jesus whispered into my ear. "You will be learning how to reach me, Meggy." The sound of my own name sent a flood of warmth throughout my flesh. "The wisdom to do this comes only through healing, and you must be ill before you can be healed." A tear streamed down my cheek with the power of his words…and I silently listened to the song of the water. "Give the song its dance," he said, *"live.* Choose to learn about life and the world around you, no matter how much you love me, no matter how much you long for me, no matter how hated you feel here in this castle. You will be lavished with strength and the faith to find me again when you choose to stay and learn. Our love will be enriched if you learn. The blessing and beauty of life will be without measure if you choose to learn. And what you learn will form the map you will use to find me in my world of light, where I dwell without fear because I am focused on love."

I touched his face again. He was so shadowed, even by the moonlight, but I could see his beauty not only by my heart but by touch. "When does it start?" I asked.

"The moment you arrived, Meggy. Sacrifice of the past brings the future."

I glanced to the cluster of moonlit trees beside the castle. I cared not to look at the castle itself. "I do not want to go back," I said.

"Everyone of faith must go through hardship," he comforted. "Darkness is necessary for the light to shine, which is one of the things you will learn. There must be hunger before there is fullness, thirst before one can be quenched, nothingness before there is everything." He kissed my hands tenderly. "I lived in a desert, I knew only hunger and thirst; I was tempted to give up, like you are tempted now. I was offended by the forces of nature."

"How did you survive?"

"By the promise of what would be. I knew I would find you, someday. You were promised to me before time began, and that promise unites us. We are truly united in spirit. It is the same promise that will give you the hope you need when you want to give up."

"I want to give up now."

"What is your offence?"

"Being without you."

"Then learn with the hope of me, knowing our love will be much stronger." He kissed my hands again, then my palms. "I must leave you now, though I will always be with you when your heart burns with love for me. I will be your rock, your memory of what is secure and founded."

"Do not go, my Jesus…"

"I must go, if I am ever to return."

I cried and he kissed me again, then took me into the castle after I looked back one last time to the heavenly moonlit land. Solemnly, he bid me farewell in my room. I drifted to sleep, still wrapped in the blanket of his love.

I awoke to a loud burst, startling me so much that I fell out of my bed and jumped to my feet. In the complete darkness I heard heavy footsteps approach me, and I knew that there were several other people in the room with me now. "Who is there?" my voice quivered.

"Who are you to ask anything of us?" shrieked the oldest hag; I recognized her voice and her movement of widened shadow. She crashed a large bucket down at my feet, cold water splashing over the sides onto my legs and the floor with a splash. "It is about time you worked for your life here," she bellowed. "You will clean the castle, you lazy creature, from top to bottom – each and every room. And remember that this is all you are worth!"

I bent down and grasped the bucket into my hands. I was afraid to ask where to start, afraid of their loud reprimands. I took the scrub brush from within the freezing water. "Ah!" screamed the younger hag, "you are spilling water on me! Go out into the hallway and scrub, you incompetent creature." I obeyed, walking through the doorway after them. "Clean and we will soon look at what you have done." I knew immediate relief in my heart when they left, though I was certain there was more to come.

Then, out of the corner of my eye, I saw a golden light. I put down the bucket and turned toward the glimmer, and saw a woman with graying hair and a soft smile look at me with pity in her eyes. "You do not have to stay here," she said. "The people who imprison you are wicked. I will help you escape."

My heart leapt with the thought of my release from this terrible darkness, of seeing light again, but I thought of my beautiful Jesus and what he had told me. The woman, her scent lingering of jasmine, took a deep breath, and I knew she was horrified by what I had endured. Her sympathy felt comforting to me now, like a bandaging cloth on a deep cut. "I am breaking with the pressure they lay upon me," I admitted.

"Then you must leave. You are free to do so. I will help you."

"I want to leave," I said, but I thought of my Jesus' words and his tender touch, and I knew that in truth his wisdom meant more to me than anything this woman could say. "But," I thoughtfully added, "I cannot follow you. The love of another is more vital to me than you, or anything you can promise." I turned away from her light as her light grew weaker until it faded completely. I knew she had been a lie.

"My love," my Jesus breathed into my ear, "I am with you always…the darkness exists to protect you. The darkness prevents you from looking into their eyes, for their gazes are lethal. If not for the darkness, you would have sunken into the belief of them."

I held him tightly, savoring the safety I felt in his great, strong arms. "Allow me to stay with you always, my love," I cried.

"You have done well," he said. "But there are more lessons that you must learn."

"What?" I asked, though he was gone as abruptly as he appeared, and I felt him no more.

I whirled around, still unable to sense him in the dark. Instead, a bird as shadowed as the darkness amongst it, landed on my left shoulder. "You will never leave this place," the bird squawked. "You are trapped, as you were yesterday and as you will be tomorrow."

I thought for a moment, my mind feeling stronger and more intent than before. "You say," I chose my words carefully, "that life will be the same for me tomorrow as it was yesterday, yet there was no mention of today."

"The window falls into more darkness," the bird said.

"But the window of today is *between* the windows of tomorrow and yesterday," I said with confidence previously foreign to me. "That means that today is the center, *the path between*, the middle road - *the way*. Today is the tunnel through which I shall find light. Today is action. Bird," I said, "I may have been trapped yesterday and I may be trapped tomorrow – *but today I am free*."

I turned away and walked out of the room and down the hall in the other direction though I could not see, in a way that I had never gone before. Darkness abounded and the threat of misstep and danger surrounded me, but I continued forth. Before long I stumbled to a stop, feeling a door in front of me. I searched for a handle and opened, falling inside.

I was met with the soft glow of candle light in a warm room, and I raised myself upon my feet. I saw the burning candle, contained upon a wide, center table, and I walked toward it as the heavy door slammed shut behind me. I hesitated, but I knew not to turn back. I took another step forward, fearlessly.

"Hello, Lady Meggy. You are free from the fears of you own mind." I stared to the old man sitting at the table, his long, flowing white hair cascading over his gentle blue robes. "Sir Lawrence," the King of the Forest said, "has not returned yet."

In that moment I remembered everything, as though a bolt of lightning struck my mind, and I knew I had to help my Knight.

***

I held my shaking hands together over the table. The King of the Forest sat across from me, his crystal eyes peering toward me. "How long has Sir Lawrence been gone?" I questioned.

"Do you not wish to know how long you were gone in the abyss yourself?" he asked. "Three days. Sir Lawrence has taken longer to establish his good character."

"Why?" I asked.

"He has not given any mind to his own ordeal," the King answered. "He has used his time in prayer for you."

My jaw lowered and my eyes widened. "He…he was why Jesus came," I breathed; "that was *his* prayer…I heard his prayer." I knew he had never left me. Tears ran down my cheeks and my lips quivered.

"Now," the King of the Forest said, "he needs *your* prayer. "He seems to be in his own maze of confusion and pain. Guilt plagues him. I am quite concerned for him." The King's eyebrows rose as he spoke.

"What does he feel guilty about?" I blurted. "He is a knight of Lord Arnulf's realm, and he saved my life."

"But what of your betrothed?"

"My betrothed is safe," I uttered, "but Sir Lawrence is not. Naturally my thoughts are with Sir Lawrence."

"Not so naturally," the old King contradicted. "How do you know that Lord Arnulf is well? Were you not brought out this way on the pretense that he was not at all well?"

I glanced down, to my folded hands upon the table. "I was," I answered softly. "On the journey, Sir Lawrence saved my life and now you tell me that he is in danger."

"You sense correctly," he said. "Possibly you were brought to Sir Lawrence's side, and not your betrothed's, for a much greater purpose. Possibly Lord Arnulf led you to the right place at the right time. Perhaps it was always Sir Lawrence that you were meant to help. Possibly no one knew this but God. Possibly…" the King of the Forest took a breath and said, "…Sir Lawrence needs to know that."

I blinked and asked, "Is that where his guilt lies?"

"His guilt most certainly comes from loving you, though you have not chosen him. His guilt also has a life of its own."

I released my hands and held them to my mouth. "He was sorrowful that the knights with him were killed when he left them to save me." I raised my gaze to see the old man nod.

"That, he was."

"Is that his guilt?"

"He is tormented by it."

"Is he sorry he saved me?"

"Never," said the old King. "I believe he felt he should have been able to do both."

"How could he have done both? How could anyone?"

The King shrugged his shoulders. "He sees himself as small because his guilt has overpowered his heart and leaves him blind to his own goodness. Show him to be the giant he is."

"How can I do that?"

"Be who you are."

"I have done that."

The elderly King shook his head though. "No you have not," he said. "You have shown him the shadow of who you are. Now, you have gained character, and character is light. He has not seen you in the light."

"Which of the shadows shall I change first?"

"Your heart must be illuminated in his eyes. He has only seen your uncertain heart but his heart, like his love and like your love, is powerful. He remembers you at every turn. His character is strengthened."

"His prayers saved me from that awful world."

"As they were meant to," the old man said. "He was out of your reach in your time of trouble because you had to build character."

"Will my character free him?" I asked.

"That is for you to find out," the King of the Forest answered before standing up from the table and leaving the room with the door open.

I took a deep breath, the air that filled my lungs was cool and soothing. In the very center of my chest grew the most passionate feeling ever to grace me. Truly I felt the grace in this inner thunder. Somehow I could not breathe a word of my love for Jesus or my experience. Never had I felt such wrenching, such pure and true love. All love before this day was comprised of shadows, the shadows I was living in. My betrothed, as little as I knew of him and as distant to me as he was, failed to bridge the distance in my heart.

My heart ached within my chest; my head burned; my hands and feet hurt. My thoughts consisted of Sir Lawrence, of how he had saved my life with his prayer and how I now wanted to save his through the love I gained.

My hands trembled; tears streamed down my face. I saw myself meeting him again, racing toward him, my long hair flowing behind me. I envisioned us leaving the castle together, free and unrestricted, unhindered and striving, purposeful and just, complete and enlightened. But above all, I longed to see him as safe as he was when we parted ways, safe by the very will and steadfastness of his mind and my Jesus. I longed for his safety with all my heart, with all my mind, and with all my soul.

When I stood up from the table I waited a moment before I could walk, for my back was stiff and my legs possessed no strength. The candle lantern continued to burn softly, fixed to the wall by the door, though shadows seemed to abound more now than when I had first entered the room. My gown, appearing much softer and lighter than it had when I was trapped with the witches, felt looser on my body from my lack of food. My fingers were numb from clutching my hands together for hours, how many had passed I could not be certain of.

I had to open the door, the one that I had come in through myself, for I had to see where it led to, now that I had found safety. Did it even exist? Was there now reality on the other side, and if so, would I find Sir Lawrence there? I would walk into the same horror I had come from, if only I could retain my memory of Jesus.

I stepped into the darkness, though a glimmer of light over my right shoulder caught my eye. Another doorway lie beyond the one I had just emerged from and was already partially open; light streamed into the hall. I approached this new doorway and courageously entered, peering to my surroundings. The room had recently been occupied, for I noticed the wrinkled papers, the bottle of ink, and the quill beside burning candles. The papers were filled with writing – *God save her,* written over and over. I took a deep breath of stifling air to steady myself, recognizing the need for objectivity in this unfamiliarity. Though I saw no one, I felt I was not alone. I heard a sudden, abrupt crash and whirled around. A man had fallen through the doorway and landed on the stone floor. I could only stand stunned, my eyes wide. Then he raised his head and looked at me.

"Sir Lawrence!" I cried, and ran toward him with my arms held out wide. "You are hurt!" And indeed it seemed so, for blood was matted in his hair, compressed to the back of his head, and the collar of his shirt was bloody while his armor was gone. Attributed to his face were streaks of blood, sweat, and mud, but though his bottom lip was swollen and bleeding, and though his cheeks were bruised and covered by short whiskers of unshavenness, his beauty was effervescent.

"Sir Lawrence," I again breathed as I rushed toward him and fell to my knees in front of him. "Where have you been?"

He laughed, and I was filled with fear because there was only mild recognition for me in his eyes and his demeanor seemed more than a little crazed. "Where have I been? Where have *you* been? You are the reason I remain alive," Sir Lawrence huffed.

He stood upon his feet, his clothes tattered, dirt-caked, and bloodied, the bulges of strength in his arms so well defined. My heart stood still, for the steadiness of his gaze paralyzed me. "My Lord," I said almost in a trance, "are you free? Are we free to leave this place?"

"No one is free," he said, inching toward my face, "and though you may be out of your prison - you are now in *mine*." I stared into his eyes as the emotion was stricken from his face. Candlelight flickered and shadows were cast through the room, lingering upon his face, deepening his eyes. I was stunned. Then over his shoulder crawled an enormous spider the size of one of my fists, its legs grasping onto his shirt. I froze, and watched as two more black spiders, just as large, crawled over his other shoulder. Still, no emotion animated his face. I held my hands to my head and screamed. The sound seemed to suddenly wake him up.

Life came into his eyes and he shouted, "Come!" He clutched my arm and yanked me roughly out of the room and into the hall. I heard the thuds of the spiders as they fell to the floor.

"No, this is the wrong way!" I screamed.

But he continued to lead me down the hall as though he had never heard me. Light abounded as we emerged from the hall and darted down a long stairway. This was not the same stairway that I had tumbled down, I realized, and this grand room, bathed in luminous light, was foreign to any darkened area that I had formerly been trapped in.

Before I could stand I saw an even brighter, blazing hot flash of light beside my face. My knight's arm covered my eyes and he brought me down to my knees where he held me tight. The growl that emulated from the light was deafening, louder than any crack of thunder. So close to me was the sound that I wondered if it were directly upon me. So intense was the sudden blast of heat that I knew I surely burned. I cried, sobbed, in awful terror.

He took my arms and pulled me up. We bolted together, running for our lives, and for our sanity.

***

I lay huddled, embraced by my knight, in a well-lit library. I did not trust this restful moment. My whole body trembled and my tears kept my face moist. I was grateful for his firm hands about me though, his soft breath in my hair.

"Are you harmed?" he asked me softly.

"What was that?" I asked. "How can light be so terrifying?"

"The light was fear itself," he answered, almost distantly. "You have just peered into the face of the dragon that haunts me."

"How can evil live in light?" I asked.

Sir Lawrence said nothing, though I glanced up to see concern for me in his eyes. I listened, comforted by his gaze in the midst of my fear, as he answered my question. "The light is the dragon's greatest tool," he said. "Light so bright can blind a man from the truth and leave him unarmed against deception."

"I do not understand," I whispered, cherishing the sound of his heartbeat as I lay my head against his chest.

"Those creatures, the ones in the light, were created when time began. Their sole purpose is to terrify. Theirs' is amongst the highest forms of light."

"That beast of fear lives in light? When I was trapped in darkness I so desperately wanted to reach light."

"Yes," he said gently but with profound wisdom, "but this is light beyond light. This is heat itself. This is the light that cleaves to God."

"Is light evil, then?"

"No," he answered, "light is never evil. Light is pure love, in its most unadulterated form. Love so pure cannot be hidden. Love must test and love must endure. But it is the cause of great fear, it is terrifying. Pure love is not for the faint of heart."

I blinked, unable to quite grasp the notion of fear within love. "But," I said, "Darkness cannot hide the light."

He kissed my brow, tenderly…like Jesus had done in the darkness. "It is possible," my knight breathed into my ear, "to be blinded by the light. It is possible to love and be loved so much that one cannot see just from unjust, one cannot see the helplessness of one's own surroundings. The nature of love is to consume, like the dragon threatens."

"If that was love," I began, "why was it so terrifying?"

"Because fear of the unknown is greater than any other fear that one can face. Fear of the unknown makes cowards out of the most courageous. Fear of the unknown is Terror itself. There is no fear greater. The threat we felt to our lives was truly our fear of the unknown, that is to say what love looks like when it takes shape – a fire-breathing dragon." My eyebrows narrowed in confusion, for my Jesus had not terrified me. "Love of the earth is covered, in a sense. Love mystifies, and that is its terror. Courage comes from uncovering the mystery and beholding what lies beneath. A man is always afraid of what he does not understand. Pure love is only for the most courageous; pure love is only for he who overcomes, for this fear of the unknown must be put down."

"Is that why you have been faced with such horrors, so that you might know the unknown?"

"To love something truly you have to know it," he said. "Now come," he bid me, raising me to my feet with him, "we have to go back into the unknown so that we may know it, otherwise it will remain our greatest source of fear. Even outside these castle walls we will be afraid of what we do not know, and we will be too afraid to go forth in our lives. We will be afraid of *each other*, and we will avoid each other." I stepped with him to the door and held him tightly as he opened it, the blinding white light shooting into my eyes like an assault of arrows.

**

When we next crashed through the library door and Sir Lawrence slammed it shut behind us, I saw that he was bleeding from his ears. "Do not go back out there – ever!" I pleaded, holding his ears with my hands. "Why is it so important to be hurt?"

"Because," he began, breathing heavily and shivering, "there is something I need, that I have to get."

"What?"

"The knowledge of you," he gasped. An ancient man, even older than the King of the Forest, then slipped through the door. I stared at him blankly, for I was not sure that he had even opened it. "Who goes there?" Sir Lawrence demanded of the stranger.

The ancient man, robed in black, his hair and his beard as white as the light, narrowed his eyes and held a long, dark, twisted staff toward my injured knight. "I am here," he boomed, "so that you might know this light and therefore overcome the fear of it."

Sir Lawrence nodded, but winced with the pain it caused. "That is what I have been trying to do," he agreed. "What has the light blinded me against? What will help me go on?"

The old man lowered his staff as the corner of his thin red lips turned up in a slight grin. "Your faith," he answered. "You will prove yourself worthy by your faith. You have been beaten, bruised, and torn by love, and now you must learn that you are worthy of love and fear will not be the master of you. Give yourself up to love, and in your sacrifice you will find that you know the King, and that his Kingdom *is* Love. By ruling love, he has become love, for there is no separateness his Kingdom. Live in love, and you will know love." His streaming beard brushed his staff with his last words. "Have faith in that."

"I am lacking faith," Sir Lawrence confessed with great understanding in his gaze. "Then it is my own lack of faith that I must overcome."

"It is your guilt you must overcome – before one can overcome, one must know," said the wizard.

"Must I know faith, even before I know love?"

"You cannot know love without knowing faith first, such a thing is impossibility. Without faith, love can be great, but it would never be felt, never trusted, and not known. You must focus on learning faith before you can learn love."

"I have rescued the Lady," my dear knight began, "though now it appears I am the one that needs to be rescued by *her*."

"Maybe so," the ancient man said, "however, do not forget the assistance you can gain from the future."

"I am not a sorcerer."

The wizard raised both full, white eyebrows. "A sorcerer believes he is a sorcerer. A friend of God believes in Truth. Be a friend to yourself instead of being your own worst enemy. By seeing into the future you have a prime opportunity to love your enemy."

"I cannot manipulate the future."

"Nor would you want to, but you can alter the pathway by filling it with love, and most of all, with the knowledge of love."

"Then how do I see into the future?"

"By looking into the eyes of the Lady," the ancient man said, and my heart stopped. "She understands what it is I am speaking of, for she herself saw into the future, when she was trapped in a world of darkness. My Lady, it is your very presence that can give life to a weary and tattered soul such as is your knight."

"Who are you? Why do you come now?" Sir Lawrence questioned.

The ancient man's quirky smile eased my heart. "Questions are pointless. You, dear knight, will live by faith because faith is for the faithful. You will find it impossible to learn faith if you were not already filled with it. This, you must know and be assured of. I have armed you with as much knowledge as is in your order to know, and now you must uncover the rest of what is hidden yourself."

"Are you leaving us?" I asked.

"Yes," the holy man answered. "I will look for you on your way out."

"What?" I asked.

"See into the future…" he said, then he slipped through the door again as mysteriously as he came in.

***

"Meggy!" Sir Lawrence shouted. "There is no time for fear – we must keep running!" my knight shouted as we ran to escape the dragon.

I cannot!" I screamed, tired to my bones upon the fear of being caught by the beast.

But as though he had not heard me at all he pulled me up by my arm and commanded, "Move!"

"I cannot!" I cried.

"If you do not move now, you never will. The fear will overtake you and we will have lost our fight. Now come!"

With surprisingly little effort I found myself running beside him, grasping his arm for balance and strength. We could not escape the ferocious fire-breathing creature….sharpened claws slammed everywhere we turned. But my knight was with me…

***

I felt the presence of love all around me, gracing over me….the love of the man named Jesus. He was so near to me. When I stretched my arm out and held my hand open, my fingers limp for touch, I wanted only to grasp his hand and tell him how undying my love for him was. I had known, with all my heart, that he would take my hand – *I knew* it before it happened.

Instantly upon taking hold of my hand, he pulled me toward him. I took a deep breath with the movement, as he kissed my face tenderly. Slowly, I opened my eyes and focused upon what was before me. Trees; green leaves; a strong, armored knight with dark hair, holding me in his arms. "Where am I?" I asked.

"You have broken us out of my prison," my knight answered. My Jesus had seeped through him to stir me to health.

"What?"

"You were attacked," he softly told me, "but you told me that no matter what happened, you knew that I would save you. You were so sure. There was no doubt at all in your eyes, and I knew in my soul that you believed I would save you no matter what happened. Then," he continued, stroking the side of my face, "I knew that faith is devout love, and devout love is faith. Your faith, and your devotion to me filled me with understanding and freed us. We are no longer held by the Castle of Wonders. We have been released into the forest, and we have our horse. We will return to our journey now, my Lady, for there is much to share with our fellow Man."

***

Deep within the forest we rode, but deep within time we seemed lost. I held tightly to Sir Lawrence's waist as we cut a narrow path through the heavy trees and brush. He said very little, as one of his hands was pressed over mine.

I gently began, "I cannot remain betrothed to the Earl."

"For now," he said, "I must return you to the Earl. It would be too dangerous for you if you are not within the realm of his royal protection. After King William conquered the English he assumed they conquered Wales as well, but the Welsh are not relenting. They fight on. The men who attacked us...and killed all my knight brothers...were the sons of Gruffyd ab Llewelyn, Welsh nationalists, and now we are in the Forest of Broceliande."

"Where is that?"

"It is in Wales," he answered. I was stunned. Then he said, "I can tell our whereabouts by the stunted growth of the trees. But we must find our way south, to Pembroke."

"How did we get so far off our course?" I asked meekly.

"The King of the Forest was not simply an old man - I have *remembered*. We may have found our way out of his Castle of Wonders, but we are still held within his realm. My Lady, we are not free. We are not safe for long." I tilted my head back and gazed into his eyes, willingly imprisoned by their dark mystery. "We must reach the Earl quickly."

In that moment I thought of my Jesus, and I said, "We were not completely at the mercy of our delusions. The old King has no power himself to change the way our surroundings appear. Our hearts do that." My knight held me more firmly in his arms as I said, "Our love has proven itself. We may appear to be in northern Wales, but truly we are nearing Pembroke." With stark clarity I felt the soldiers of Jesus in our minds, like haunting figures at first, ghosts emerging from the fog, freeing us from the land that was not. I knew now that things were not always as they seemed. I sighed with relief when the trees seemed taller.

Sir Lawrence sighed also, lowering his head. "You have saved us again," he said. Then he grew quiet, and I knew his thoughts were deep so I did nothing to disturb him. We rode along a more familiar forested road now, but without speaking. I sensed his foreboding; we would soon meet Lord Arnulf. I would no longer marry the Earl, but Sir Lawrence must have felt the responsibility for my decision. In truth, I did not know the Earl. Yet, I dreaded telling him that I would never be his wife. I could not let go of my knight.

***

I was exhausted, but I clung to my knight as we rode toward the timber and earth buildings and homes that comprised Pembroke. We both knew the difficult chore that awaited me within the town. My knight did not prompt our horse to move more swiftly, and I felt he treasured these last moments alone with me. His gaze often met mine, whether we rode beside a steadily flowing stream or were searching for our way amidst faith in a forest maze.

I felt as though we neared our deaths when we rode into the city. The people that bustled through the streets and between buildings under an overcast sky were like the shadows of a dream. I could hear only the constant murmur of citizens as Sir Lawrence veered our horse onto another road, toward the castle in the center of the city. I buried my head behind the vest of his armor, lifting my gaze only to see the goats and pigs that noisily crossed our path and the shouting herder that followed them. The road in which we traveled was narrow, and the small, tightly packed houses were often anchored by a butcher's shop or craftsman's shop. The upper levels of the dwellings served as canopies for the streets, making good use of little area. A flock of geese waddled beside our horse for several strides.

And again, we were engulfed by a shadow. I looked up; we were in the center of the small town now, before the walls of the castle. I felt his chest grow as he took a deep breath and prompted our horse nearer. Just outside the wall was the charred frame of a Priory chapel, the inward edges of its walls black, its interior completely gutted. My heart felt shattered, for I had remembered my townspeople speaking of the promise in Monkton Priory. Lord Arnulf had been planning to serve as the catalyst of a new world of knowledge and wisdom, through the monks and their Priory which had in years past been a Celtic Christian community. He had promised his citizens that the only way to be free of the oblivion of war was to fill the mind with knowledge, because if Mankind knew the secrets and beauty of the world as God wanted Him to know them, He would be too hesitant to harm it. I gazed now upon the wonder of what would have been a white-washed Priory building and envisioned the monks, all clothed in dark robes, cradling manuscripts in their arms, moving freely past the grand wooden doors. "I wanted to tell you about the fate of the secret university that would be formed within the Priory many times but I could not, for your safety," Sir Lawrence turned slightly to tell me. "It burned last month, by those who wished to destroy knowledge and its prosperity."

"By those who attacked us on the road the day you saved me?"

"Yes," he said, "and the Earl is inside the castle walls. Anselm, the Archbishop of Canterbury, reports to him daily about the progress of the secret university. Our intent is to rebuild this Priory and unite England in knowledge under its guise, for it will be the seat of wisdom." Though his eyes were shadowed by the day, they glistened and warmed my heart.

"Has he truly been injured?" I asked, holding back from asking more.

My knight nodded, still appearing forlorn to me. "When he heard the Priory had burned his heart broke. You will see a changed man; he will not be the same man you were told of…the man to whom you are betrothed. He survives now only by hope."

When we reined our horse up at the Priory, and I peered to the modest, though singed buildings that surrounded an inner courtyard, my gaze lingered upon a figure clothed in a long brown robe, standing between two doorways. Sir Lawrence unintentionally nudged me as he dismounted from the horse, then he raised his arms to help me slide off as well. I peered into his eyes, for we both knew who the robed man was. I had to turn away from my knight, toward the Priory, for I felt the obligation of duty; I could tell Lord Arnulf the truth later. He turned toward me, his brown robe shifting as he came nearer. I stepped swiftly toward him. "Are you injured, my Lord?" I questioned softly.

"Come," he said deeply, holding an opened hand toward me, "Come inside, my child, my betrothed." I noticed wisps of shoulder-length hair, grey with age, beneath a hood which shadowed his worn face. His eyes bore the omniscient mastery of responsibility.

I took his hand as he looked past me to speak to my knight: "I am in your debt forever, Sir Lawrence. You have delivered Lady Meggy to me safely." The Earl then so swiftly pulled me away that I had not the chance to gaze to my knight with the longing that struck my heart.

He led me into one of the surrounding rooms that had not been damaged by fire, sparsely furnished with a bed and a chair that creaked as the Earl sat down upon it. "I am so happy to see you, my Lord," I said graciously. I stared to him when he took his hood down, for he seemed to have aged immensely; even his gait seemed marred by strain. He met my eyes, though his were bloodshot and swollen from an obvious lack of sleep. My heart went out to him, for war had taken its toll.

"We have not been together often," he said with deep understanding his voice, "and yet I know there is something different about you, Lady Meggy. What could that be? You are withdrawn in your spirit." His solid body promised the vigor due an Earl; and though he appeared tired and worn of heart and mind, his Norman shoulders were broad and his great height made me feel smaller than I was. I lowered my head without answering. I shuddered to be so near such a powerful man as he. Gruffly, he said, "I have missed you."

With heightened anxiety I told him, "Your knights told me that you were injured."

"I *am* injured," he grumbled. "They destroyed *me* when they destroyed the Priory, which will be our university. But it will be rebuilt, greater than ever – that is my mission."

"Who are 'they'?"

"The Welsh continue to battle my forces at every turn. The Priory will not only be *our* victory, but a victory of the world." He drew a labored breath to continue, "The Priory School will be open to all. Priests, scholars, physicians, scientists – *all, secretly.* Theology will be chief among the sciences, and all thoughts will be welcomed and explored."

"You will be giving England a gift, my Lord, but why do you tell me now?"

Arnulf grinned warmly. "The Archbishop of Canterbury will be my assistant, especially once the school is in use. I must return to battle," he revealed, "and I have decided to leave Anselem, and Sir Lawrence, in charge of building." I nodded, my lips compressed. He looked at me wisely, with great strength in his eyes. "You will not accompany me," he said. "Your presence with me would be far too dangerous. But it is no longer safe for me here. Sir Lawrence took excellent care of you in my absence, for I know of the challenges that you both had to face." I felt stunned; the blood drained from my face. "He never allowed danger to creep near you," the Earl said, "and I am certain he will do the same here." He laid both of his great hands upon mine and added, "You will be able to watch the construction of a great Priory in safety. It is I, who am not safe."

I lowered my eyes and softly sighed, saying, "I do not understand any of this….but there is one thing I must tell you, about Sir Lawrence and myself…you see, though I love you like my father I do not know you well."

"No need for worry, we shall re-unite soon," he tried to re-assure me as he held my chin up with his fingers. "Until we do though, you will not be alone."

***

Rain overshadowed the day, drops hard and long, seeping through cracks, pelting onto rooftops, lasting well into the evening. Branches whipped the outside castle wall as I knelt to pray inside the chapel, two lit candles shifting light subtly before my eyes. The windows had been boarded up in an early attempt to keep out the storm, yet I prayed as though God were my only defense. I was alone among the monks as they streamed past me in their daily silence, unaffected by the turmoil outside.

The chapel door abruptly swung open, letting in a gust of wet wind and deafening thunder; I raised my head; a few of the monks turned to see what had happened. It was my knight who stood before me, the mystery of his dark eyes silently calling me to him, as another man with light hair stood next to him. Both men were soaked with rain; both men pushed the door shut again with all their strength. My heart had stopped; I could not breathe. My knight turned toward me again when the door was closed, his stunned gaze revealing that he was as overwhelmed by the sight of me as I was with him. I stood up, smoothing the skirt of my dress without thinking.

"We must act quickly, Lady," said the blond, robed man with my knight. He was not as tall as Sir Lawrence, nor was his gaze as piercing, but he did seem purposed in being in the castle chapel. He stood firmly in place, rainwater dripping from both men, small puddles forming at their boots. The smell of rain and mud plagued me.

My knight must have seen how confused I was, for he stood taller and stared into my eyes as though to hold me up by sight. Motioning to the man beside him, he said, "This is Archbishop Anselem. He has come to help guide our plans for Monkton Priory."

Anselem, a fair man wearing a simple monk's robe, nodded politely even while soaking wet. He seemed very stoic, for he never shifted in his stance, nor did his movements seem hesitant or unsure. He must have been the same age as Lord Arnulf, for deep in his eyes rest the same haggard weariness that I had seen in the Earl's eyes. A touch of darker hair at his temples bestowed him with a look of wisdom that was expected in a teacher, though the deep creases beside his light eyes seemed to reveal the struggle he tried to conceal. He did not appear as strong in body as my knight, nor as resolute. But there was something reassuring about him, something in his spirit that was not quite as distant as his appearance would suggest. "Lady Meggy," Anselem addressed, "my loyalties, as always, reside with Lord Arnulf. He has told me about the Priory School he intends to build, and he told me that you must first approve of my plans, as well as the curriculum that I will teach."

"Me?" I questioned. "I know nothing of schools, or teachers, or scholars. Such a duty must be left in the more capable hands of Sir Lawrence." I glanced into the deep, dark eyes of my knight with complete trust.

"As you wish," Anselem said, and for the first time I noticed a slight French accent lingering in his words. "However, the Earl requests that your opinion be recognized."

I lowered my head and sighed, for I was overwhelmed. "I will not know what to say. Though my heart may speak, my lips are conditioned to remain still in matters of State."

"Yet -" Anselem said, "Now is the time to bring the decision makers and peace keepers of the world together with God's purposeful education."

"A new time calls for a new order?" I asked.

"That is right," Anselem agreed. He drew his leather gloves off and blew on his hands to warm them.

"This is what the Earl wants, my Lady," Sir Lawrence said, bowing to me slightly. His gesture, though gallant, felt odd.

***

A few days had gone by without seeing Sir Lawrence, and though the sky was dark with drizzling rain I rode under a heavy black cape toward the Priory outside the castle wall, where I expected to secretly meet Archbishop Anselem and my knight. The streets were much less crowded this morning, my horse splashing in puddles of rain water as he stepped, the stench of waste from small herds of sheep turning my stomach. A mother and her young daughter, mud from the road clinging to the hemlines of their dresses, walked dreamily after a flock of cackling hens. Then I lifted my gaze to the grandeur that would be the Priory school, for the modest arches had begun to shape place.

The burnt-out building appeared vacant of working men. I wondered if I could locate anyone; I peered from side to side, my cloak's hood brushing my cheeks with my movement. I saw no one working on the building outside, either. I reined my horse beneath a nearby overhang to escape the rain that had grown above the drizzle it had been when I first left for a short ride. A shadow overtook me, regardless of the impatient stepping of my horse.

Finally I saw two men riding at a prance on the narrow road toward me, one wearing a blue cloak and the other man wearing a black cloak. In only moments they had approached me. The man in the darkest cloak, his face shadowed by his hood, said, "Follow us." His voice struck my heart immediately, for it was as familiar as my own.

I rode beside the darker cloaked man, for though his identity was hidden I had no doubt of who he was. I reined into the alleyway behind him. He dismounted from his horse, then stepped toward me to help me slide down as well; I saw the man wearing the blue cloak dismounting also from the corner of my eye.

My knight grasped my waist tightly, I felt faint. Then he carefully released me and nudged me forward. "Where are you taking me?" I asked, sheltered from the drizzle by the overhang of a dwelling. I longed to be in the forest alone with him, learning in the castle or on the wooded trail again.

"Inside here," he said softly, leading me toward the nearest dark wooden door.

"A tobacco shop?" I asked, for the rich scent of tobacco lingered even in the rain.

He met my gaze and led me inside. A deep shadow enveloped us upon entering the room and seemed to follow us as we walked further inside. Then we climbed a staircase in the back, in a narrow space behind the hearth in which a lit fire was glowing. I heard footsteps behind us though I did not look as we stepped up, for my knight briskly led me through another door. My eyes were drawn to the crowd of six men who sat around a simple, round wooden table, all turning immediately toward me. "Sit down," Sir Lawrence said, motioning to the three empty chairs at the table. By the stern expression upon his face, I knew something serious was meant to take place.

Careful not to disrupt the men at the round table, I slipped into the chair designated for me, followed by my knight who sat in the chair beside me. Anselem sat in the chair next to Sir Lawrence and removed his blue cloak, glistening with rain drizzle. He glanced toward me also, stark realism upon his face, then I looked to my knight. I wondered what my knight's thoughts were, why he led me into the room that fronted as a tobacco shop, and why he sat beside me now.

"Men - Knights," Sir Lawrence addressed the men, all camouflaged as peasants in simple clothes, "this is Lady Meggy with your knight brother Anselem." He was not only an Archbishop.

"Indeed," the man across from me agreed, his hair gray with wrinkles on his face. "Truly," agreed the younger brown-haired man beside him. "It is our greatest honor to have you with us, Lady Meggy."

"As it is mine," I answered, "but I will not..."

Sir Lawrence stood from his chair, his commanding presence all but stopping my heart. "The duty has befallen us, a handful of men," my Knight began, "to do God's work. Though we are few in number and the secrecy of our duty is great, we are burdened with this mission. We will carry out what Lord Arnulf has called upon us to do, for it is what God has called upon *him* to do. Gentlemen," he addressed, then glanced toward me, "and Lady, we begin God's Unity on earth, for as Unity is brought forth only with knowledge, knowledge itself is our purpose. We have begun rebuilding the Priory, in body as in soul, where *all* may come to drink in God's knowledge."

All six men at the table, besides Sir Lawrence and myself, nodded. I bit my bottom lip; my hands were numb as I wrung them in my lap. I confessed, "I do not see how I can help you in this great endeavor."

The old man laughed, though I recognized the respect in his gaze. "Most of those called by God have said the very same thing," he said.

Sir Lawrence sat back in his chair, though Anselem stood up, his arms to his sides, and cleared his voice. "Faith is a choice," he said. "Must we believe in order to think, which is the basis of all humanity? The truth is revealed – hold fast to it, as we all must."

"There is truth in your words," the only man whom had not yet spoken up said. He sat on the other side of my knight and appeared to be not yet in his twenties, for his hair was evenly light brown and his face was smooth.

"However," Sir Lawrence interjected, "it is the Question itself that will lead Mankind forth. The Question prompts Him to search for Truth, and where would the world be without Seekers of the Answer? Sirs," he held eye contact with all of them at certain points as he addressed them, his hands upon the table as he leaned forward, "you say there is only one absolute truth and reality, and though this may be true the world would continue to be thrown into turmoil if not for those who seek. Seekers provide balance and equip with inertia. Let us provide the seekers in the secret school of the Priory by allowing them the freedom to stretch their minds. Let there be no boundaries to our curriculum. Let exceptional minds come there to seek answers. And let them never be content in finding, for the inquisitiveness prompted by doubt must never be hindered. Much would be lost to the world without doubt, Sirs."

"Nor fear," I said under my breath. I compressed my lips and looked up into the faces of the men, their eyes all trained on me.

"True," my knight said, slapping the table hard with his hands. "Fear," he said, convicted, "is the very bridge of knowledge and understanding, for without it questions would not be drawn together to yield theories. Fear is not a devil, it is an angel in disguise, as are all angels."

"I will atone to that," said Archbishop Anselem, and his blue eyes met mine. I glanced down to the dark wood table.

"Our Lady is the very foundation of the university," Sir Lawrence said, his voice striking my soul. Then he looked to me and said, "It is time that you knew your destiny."

"Sir Lawrence," the old knight interjected, "she is not ready for it."

"She must know her value."

"No!" I shrieked, quickly bursting away from the table and turning from them all. I thought I heard a few of the man call after me, but I ran out of the room, down the stairs, and out of the would-be-tobacco shop. Gratefully, there was no longer any drizzle so I did not miss my cloak, but I had only just rounded the muddy cobblestone corner when I crossed the path of a mother as she taught her young daughter.

The mother, her sandy-colored hair pulled up behind her head with several loose strands having gone awry in the moist air, sat on a stool outside a shop door. Her young daughter, wearing a light blue peasant's dress like her mother, listened closely, her delicate eyes following every move her mother made. I rubbed my arms for warmth and listened as well.

"Fin MacCool was a great giant," the mother said. "He had integrity, wisdom, and discipline, dear child. He was chosen by the King for his great strength and courage to lead an army. But dear girl, he was above all, a teacher. You must learn the message of his story. Words are like veils, and what we think is said is mystical. That's Fin MacCool, a truth hidden beneath stories; the stories are like veils….Demna peered into a fish to see the future."

"Who is Demna?" the girl innocently asked.

"Demna is Fin MacCool's endeared name."

"What fish showed him the future?"

"The fish, child," the mother said gently, "Means wisdom."

"He ate wisdom? I am sure he must have eaten the fish."

"He *listened* to wisdom and understood it. He may have listened as his mother taught him, like you do."

Someone suddenly whispered in my ear, "Where do you think this legend that she's telling her daughter came from?" My heart stopped and my cheeks flushed, and I looked up to see my knight gazing into my eyes. "I'll tell you…" he continued to whisper, his breath hot against my neck. "Fin MacCool and his army were Christ and his disciples, just among a different culture. That is what the secret Priory knowledge will introduce.

Not everyone and not all cultures can understand the same version of the story, so there are legends. Histories need to be taught and clarified."

I realized that I had been biting my bottom lip until it was numb, for I felt calmed with the tone of his voice. "I do not understand why I must be so involved," I whispered, "and why you cannot move ahead without me. What do I have that you need?"

"The story that this woman is telling her daughter has a lot to do with the reason we need you. The Priory is being created *around* you, though you may not know it." The confusion that overcame me was evident on my tensed brow, for Sir Lawrence took me into his arms tightly. He brought me back into the alleyway and brushed the loose strands of my hair out of my eyes. He leaned down, his lips close to my ear, and whispered, "You are the foundation upon which the secret Priory school is being built. Now, let us go back among the knights, where we will reveal all to you. I give you my word." I nodded, for I trusted him with my life. He led me carefully and swiftly into the tobacco shop again, then up the stairs and into the hidden room.

"Ah!" Archbishop Anselem commended as I entered, "you have returned, now we shall get back to business."

"Wait-" my knight told the men at the round table, "We must speak directly."

"As you wish," the gray-haired knight said.

"My Lady," Sir Anselem began, "the Earl has entrusted us to rebuild the Priory, and with *you*." My knight helped me into a chair, then pulled his chair nearer to mine and sat down beside me. I folded my hands in my lap and listened to Anselem. "The school that we are to create within the Priory," he continued, "will teach all that has been taught before, but we will also encourage and foster new ideas that are creative...*original*. This can only be done through the faith that God has given each person a purpose. We will help uncover that purpose."

"Purpose in God?" I asked.

"We will encourage, shall we say, logical proof of God's will."

"But," I began meekly but was encouraged by my knight's attentive gaze, "what is the logical proof of God? Are we not to believe by faith?"

"Faith leads to logic," Anselem answered. "Realism implies the comfort of God, which comes from recognizing Him as all – as Love."

"Archbishop Anselem gets ahead of himself," the youngest knight said.

"Yes, he does," my knight affirmed.

"It is difficult not to when there is so much understanding to be had in such little time," Anselem said.

"And truly this is the reason and need of a Priory school – *timely understanding*," the young knight added.

"Understanding," said Anselem, "is reached through gratitude…gratitude for knowledge and gratitude for life itself, because with knowledge a person is more aware of *why* life is meant to be held in such gratitude. That, my Lady, is why the Earl has requested our services in the construction of the Priory school."

"Yes," agreed the eldest knight as he straightened his back and fixed his gaze on mine. "And you are to awaken that gratitude, my Lady. You see, as Christ died on the cross, his banner will always wave in the breeze of love. *You* are the banner we have sought, my Lady. And yet, the Earl is not the breeze that awakens you. There is another who has done that."

I lowered my head in confusion. The knight called Simon said, "That is why we look to you, Lady."

"It is time for you to raise your banner."

"You were born to it," Sir Lawrence said quickly as though trying to catch me with his words.

I abruptly questioned, "You are saying, then, that I am the banner you seek? Is that why you protected me so dearly, Sir Lawrence? I am your mission?"

"I have not taken good care of you, my Lady, or we would never have been deterred."

"And I thought all the knights were killed!" I shrieked.

"We had to make it appear so," Sir Christoff, in whose guidance my journey had begun, walked in through the door and said. "We have blurred the truth, but in order to set the minds of Mankind free."

"I do not know what to think," I admitted.

"Why did you come back with me?" my knight asked me. "*I am* the wind that lifts your banner. We have to admit the truth. There is too much at stake."

"Starving the heart feeds the soul," Anselem said, "the mind thrives on suffering, but to spread the knowledge love must be the catalyst. What you do not know will return to you when the time arises," he continued, "for it will be your memory that reveals. Memory is often illusive until there is need for it. But it is the illusion that keeps it strong…by nature it has to overcome misunderstanding – and this is where it gains its greatest strength. Mankind must withstand his own doubt."

Sir Lawrence's gaze had never broken from mine, no matter who had spoken. "I have suffered for the both of us," he said softly.

"Sacrifice brings knowledge," Anselem promised. "The knight has sacrificed his own heart in love for you, dear Lady. Now is the time for us, brothers, to be patient and have faith."

***

I quickly left the room and mounted my horse, and without waiting for Sir Lawrence I raced toward the chapel within the castle walls. There, I found a solitary pew and sat alone; sunlight separated into colored shards as it pierced the stained glass window, and I bowed my head.

I was praying when I heard a crash; I lowered my hands and looked up. I turned around and was startled to see that the door had been flung open upon itself – and Lord Arnulf, the Earl of Pembroke, stood alone, his ever-commanding presence prevalent in the doorway. He was clothed in a monk's brown robe again and he seemed somewhat unsteady. "My Lord," I uttered. I then stood and bowed.

"Lady Meggy," he huffed; I looked up to see the strain in his usually stoic eyes and the exhaustion upon his crinkled brow.

"What has happened?" I asked. I peered toward him, anxiously awaiting answers about his tired state.

He did not conceal his wince as some of his gray hair fell in front of his eyes. "I must tell you that I am injured," he announced. "I have been injured for quite some time, even before I saw you last. My wound will not heal."

I began to rush toward him, asking, and "How bad is it? Where are you injured?"

The Earl took a labored breath and lowered his head. He smelled of sweat and the grime of forest road travel. "My wound," he began, "is in my stomach. When the Priory was set ablaze last, I would have given my life to save it - my wound from that effort is not healing."

"Why do you travel? Rest, and let the monks heal you!" I pleaded.

The Earl simply shook his head, though. "Thank you, my Lady," he said, "but I have called upon the best physicians in England. They all agree that my wound will not heal, so I have decided to go on about my days as long as God's wills them to last. My only concern is how the Priory is progressing."

"How can you think about that when you are so hurt?" I cried.

"A constant hunger bleeds through me. So please, give me news about the Priory. How are my knights?"

"They do well," I answered. "All is progressing well."

His grey eyebrows rose. "You know this?" he asked. "That means you are involved in the school and my prayer has been answered. It is this feeding of knowledge that will heal my unhealing wound."

"Please rest, my Lord," I said softly.

"Did they tell you the truth?" he asked.

I could not help taking a step back. "You knew?" I asked quietly.

Lord Arnulf nodded. "What they say is true. Christ's banner is your heart, my Lady, you must believe this. You must understand and accept the responsibility that accompanies knowing this."

"Why did they have to tell me" I asked, "why could you not tell me? Why must it have been so mysterious?"

"It would have been taken away or you would have been hurt if everyone knew about the Priory school. And…" he added, "One of my knights is the breeze that waves your banner." I looked deep into his eyes for any sort of consolation but found none. Instead he added, "I needed to be assured of which of my knights God has chosen to help you."

"My Lord," I began.

But he waved his hand before me and said, "There is joy in re-fitting pieces that were once joined at the beginning of time, like the artist who pieces his masterpiece together after an accident. He is more proud of it than he had been originally," he continued, "and you cannot doubt the Earl of Pembroke. Accompany me to the Priory. I want to see the construction with you."

"Will you heal when the Priory school is finished and the banner of Christ blows?"

"I will heal, for my duty will be fulfilled. I will go to the land of my youth, reserved only for royalty, for I will have seen the fruit of my labor and be blessed. My Lady, you have asked the question that will heal me."

***

When I rode well past the gates of Pembroke castle the next afternoon I was met with overpowering screams. I reined my horse up, my gaze darting in every direction in my effort to understand what was happening. "The Welsh have come!" a boy looked up to me upon my horse and shouted. "Lord Arnulf is here somewhere and they are looking for him!"

I carefully tugged upon the hood of my cape to be sure that my face was hidden, then I reined my horse toward the small shop on the corner. I held my breath as a crowd of men ran past me. I knew where they were going.

I slid down off my horse; the street I stepped into was still soggy from the season of steady rain; I looked up to see white smoke rising from a distant building. The clouds were much less imposing, though doubt and confusion shadowed my mind and heart. I knew I must find Sir Lawrence quickly to learn how to escape the chaos. I had tried to tie up my horse but he ran in the commotion.

Someone strong took hold of my upper arm. I peered over my shoulder and caught my breath. My knight's dark, looming eyes gaze reached into mine; I felt my very spirit saved. "Is the Earl at the Priory?" he whispered.

"No," I answered just as quickly, "He left before the sun rose this morning."

My knight sighed with relief. "Good," he said. "The Welsh intend to do him harm if they find him." I nodded, for I understood the threat to his safety. "They have set fire to Pembroke already but our knights and the citizens have extinguished the flames and saved the Priory."

"What do I do?" I asked, though in the chaos I was not sure he heard me.

"You can do nothing. It has begun…the Earl will go on his way," he breathed into my ear, "hidden from the masses until the need arises."

"What need?" I asked, my confusion twisting my stomach.

"The need of all humanity, with true love. But the Earl has chosen *his* day, and this is the beginning." I nodded, and Sir Lawrence added, "He wishes us to continue with the construction of Monkton Priory no matter what takes place. The army will destroy the Welsh."

My knight held my waist and led me through the alarmed crowd, toward the castle. For the first time, as we sifted through the people and turmoil, I felt the supreme duty that was ours.

***

"I am glad, and relieved, that you believe us," Archbishop Anselem said to me. I looked around the small room that Sir Lawrence had led me into, deep amid the hidden catacombs beneath the Priory. We had been slowly walking for an hour and I was tired, and yet I sensed that our journey was not over yet. The dark earth itself formed the walls and floor and ceilings about us now, the smell of drudged earth overwhelmed me, as flaming torches were our only source of light. I looked to my side, past my knight, and saw Anselem seated upon an earthen bench with a book opened in his hands and several balanced on his lap. He looked up to me, and I realized that in the torch light he looked much older than his years. "The time has come to reassure you of the order in our deeds."

"Why must you reassure me?" I asked quickly. "I know what you have said, that I am the banner of Jesus - but do we all not have a Christ within us?"

"Not like you," Anselem answered, his gaze unwavering. The banner that you carry is his blood and faith. You are descendant of Mary's ancient bloodline. Lord Arnulf was told in a dream. Lady Meggy, it is of great importance that you accept this knowledge."

My knight squeezed my arm as though to remind me of his strength, and that he would hold me up. I believed in my knight. I asked, "What must I do with it?"

"She accepts," Anselem said somewhat jubilantly. He looked into my eyes to tell me, "You are the truth of God, and you must enlighten others." My heart stopped, for I wondered if this was another reason that Jesus had come to me in the Forest Castle. He must have been leading me to the Priory…in Sir Lawrence's arms. Anselem looked introspective then and added, his fingers to his chin, "You must not go backward in your knowledge. Move forward only. You are Truth. Sir Lawrence's love has awakened you, and the Forest Castle awakened you. Before that, you were living in your sleep. But *now* you will know the truth in each cornerstone of the Priory, and you will pass knowledge onto others."

I looked toward my knight, blurting, "That is why you watched me before I knew you…"

"Among other reasons," he answered. "This you must hear, my Lady, for you are not only the Truth, but you now become the Story. It is by your life that the story will flow."

"Are you in the flow, like you are in the wind?" I questioned.

"There is no one greater," Anselem said, "and there is no one lesser. All are equal in the eyes of God, all creeds and all wisdom. Water is only water until it has been blessed, then it can be called holy water. You, dear Lady, have become holy through love, and this is the knowledge that the world must learn. The Priory school will prepare its students for this wisdom through knowledge, vast as an ocean. Each student will be armed with a shield and sword of knowledge."

I sighed deeply. My knight quickly embraced me as though he were holding me up. "How can just one school benefit the whole of Mankind?" I asked, my lips brushing against the coarse vest over his chainmail armor.

"By preparing the way," Anselem answered. "The Priory school is God's herald."

"Should the world not be filled with schools such as these to prosper?"

"The world must have an example to follow, an original thought to carry on. And that is what the Priory itself will encourage – *original thought*. It will be the model of others to come in all different lands. Once it is completed, scholars will study there and broaden their minds – as was Christ's simple life and example…finding perfect joy in a mind perfectly free in understanding. First, understanding and love must unite to bring this into fulfillment. Knowledge you found in the forest castle fills you, and because of this you are the banner that announces the coming of Jesus. With Sir Lawrence's love you are the banner that waves. You ask me what you must do and I tell you that you are to live the Truth." I held onto my knight tightly, his armor cold and pressed against my cheek. Anselem continued, "Love is the only way a person can be free enough to embrace knowledge. With love, a person's defenses are down and truth may enter. Love is the bridge, love is the adjoining street, and love links the giver to the receiver. Truth is the vehicle that moves between the links. Knowledge is the blood of Christ. A person must be open to allow it to fully spill over in the mind. I am pointing you away from the opportunities that formally lay before you and ask you to let down your walls and believe."

My mouth hung ajar, for I was stunned and moved by Anselem's words. "What must I do?" I asked. "What must I say?"

"Say nothing," answered Archbishop Anselem, "for silence is wisdom's greatest virtue. It is never simple. The simpler this quest appears, the more difficult it is in truth. *Truth* is what we seek. Simplicity serves as God's veil." Anselem raised his shadowed hand to his head, brushing his hair lightly back between his fingers. Then, his hand falling to his lap upon the closed books, he added, "Complexity proves the existence of God, for through complexity a person may find several paths to Truth and to God."

I raised my head off Sir Lawrence's chest, and stood strongly on my own. I nodded meaningfully. "I understand," I said.

"Then dear Lady," Anselem said gently, "you must allow this knowledge to have a home within you, accept it into your understanding. Return to the castle chapel now and pray. The school, and I, will still be here tomorrow, prepared to fulfill our mission."

When my knight led me through the tunnels again and back into the Priory itself, Anselem stayed behind. I dared not ask why, though I knew I could. Instead, I was silent as Sir Lawrence led me through the great doors, then to mount his horse.

***

My long, golden hair flew beside my face in the wind, and I leaned further back into the chest of my knight. We rode past a wide oak tree beside the road, past the shops of Pembroke, toward the white stone gate of the Priory. I feared going inside as the builders worked, though I knew I feared the Unknown.

"I have loved you since long before you knew who I was," my knight whispered into my sun-draped ear. I was indeed grateful for the steady warmth of a cloudless afternoon.

"That was a different time," I said, though I was limp in his arms.

"One time leads to the next."

"And now we prosper the mission of a Priory. We are meant to receive God, my knight. I *want* to receive; I will fulfill my life's purpose. Our love is mirrored by the growth and success of the Priory school. I did not know that until I looked into your eyes today. I am aware of the importance of our lessons. We are more than architects – we are *historians*."

"That, we are," my knight said. We continued on our gentle, sun-guided path toward the Priory alone, though we would never be apart again.

The End